CHANGE OF FORTUNE

FORTUNE CHRONICLES 2.5

KATHLEEN MCCLURE
KELLEY MCKINNON

PUBLISHED BY OUTRAGEOUS FICTION

***This Work was originally published under the title *The Crew Who Came in From the Cold*.**

Edited by Lori Diederich
Cover by Youness Elh
ISBNs:
978-1-947842-25-0 (eBook)
978-1-947842-30-4 (Paperback)

Thank you for choosing *Change of Fortune*.

If you enjoy the journey, please consider leaving an honest review. For individual creators like Kelley and I, your feedback is the best way to help other fans of quirky science fantasy discover our worlds.

And for more outrageous fiction, including new stories, exclusive content, and reader community, scan the QR code below to follow our Outrageous Crew on Ream. It's free, easy, and the best way to delve into our fantastical worlds!

Happy reading,

Kathleen & Kelley

https://reamstories.com/outrageouscrew

To everyone fighting to live as their true selves.

EPIGRAPH

Leave your past on the ground, lest it weigh you down.

— COLONIAL AIR CORPS MOTTO

What's past is prologue…

— WILLIAM SHAKESPEARE

PRELUDE

Jagati slouched in her chair, took another sip of the Rigging's nutty ale, and watched Eitan wend his way to the pub's excuse for a dance floor, only belatedly realizing that his desertion had left her alone with John.

She briefly wondered if he'd done it on purpose, but turning back to see him sliding into the dance, she figured Eitan was simply being Eitan and relaxing in his own way.

Given the hornet's nest of their last job, everyone on the crew could use some relaxation.

Even now, Jagati had trouble believing their struggling freight company had ended up at the center of an illegal tech scheme.

They'd come out of it okay, and in the keepers' good graces, but they hadn't come out of it unscarred.

She rubbed the side of her leg, where the bandage itched, and glanced back to Eitan, who had found himself a dance partner.

"Think she'll take him home?" she asked John.

He followed her gaze towards their crewmate. "If she doesn't, half the pub will be following him back to the *Errant*."

She grunted her agreement, then turned her glass around on itself a few times.

"So—" he began.

"I think we should—" she said at the same time.

They both stopped. "You first," he said.

"Ugh." She stopped turning the glass and rapped her knuckles on the table as she considered the conversation she, John, and Eitan had just finished. "It's just, all that talk about sensing and emotions and that minute in the cargo bay and . . ." Her voice clogged as she recalled the moment she and John had kissed—and what a kiss it had been. Then she hissed and shook her head. "Listen, sure, for kids like Rory and Jinna, it's simple," she said, referring to their mechanic and the young woman he'd been secretly pining over for years. Thankfully, Rory had taken Jinna and his starry-eyed self back to the *Errant*, leaving the grownups to enjoy their evening in peace.

"Young they may be," John countered, "but Rory and Jinna are both seasoned veterans and have lived a life. And Jinna is carrying a child of her own, under what could best be termed trying circumstances. I can't think of anything less simple."

"Yes. Fine. Whatever," Jagati admitted, waving her hand. "But they're still both younger than we are."

"Yes, they are." He almost smiled, and she almost punched him. "Which I suppose means we have less time to waste."

"Exactly! Wait." Jagati frowned. "That's not what I meant."

"Oh?" He raised his glass and took a drink before asking, "And what did you mean?"

She bared her teeth. "Sometimes I hate you."

"I know." This time he did smile, then leaned in so they were face to face, close enough to smell his soap.

She really liked his soap.

She cleared her throat. "So . . . about the queen being in my net," she began, referring to another conversation they'd had, this one a few days ago, regarding their relationship.

Or, rather, their relationship post The Kiss. It was during this conversation that John had told Jagati the next move, should there be one, was hers to make.

"Yes?" he prompted.

She stared, huffed out a breath. "I think I might keep it."

His right brow rose. "I don't know what that means."

Her eyes narrowed. "You aren't going to make this easy for me, are you?"

"It's not easy for me," he admitted, his own huff of breath displacing a curl that had fallen to her cheek. Then he reached up to brush it back, and Jagati was so shocked she didn't even slap his hand away. "I want to know what you want," he said softly.

"I thought I was being clear."

He tipped his head, indicating this was not, in fact, the case.

"I want . . ." Another huff of air. "I want—"

"Excuse me."

At the diffident greeting, John and Jagati both sat up straight as cadets in basic to see they had company, in the way of an older man whose coat was as weathered as his copper skin.

"I apologize if I'm interrupting," the man said.

"Oh, you're not interrupting," Jagati piped up.

"Of course not," John said.

"Nothing happening here," she added.

"I see." The man's expression twitched with amusement. "In that case, might I ask if I have the pleasure of addressing Captain Pitte of the *CAS Errant*?"

"Only if you're not planning on thrashing him," Jagati said.

"I'm Captain Pitte," John told the stranger. "How can I help you, Msr...?"

"Doctor, in fact," the man introduced himself with a slight bow. "Doctor Alain Natsiq, and I'm in need of an airship. I was told you might have one to hire?"

John looked at Jagati. She sighed and nodded.

"That we do," John said to the doctor. "How may the *Errant* serve?"

CHAPTER 1

"HOW MAY THE *ERRANT* SERVE?"

It wasn't the first time Jagati had heard John ask that question, but it was the first time she'd heard it with mixed emotions.

Plus side, they could use the cash a new job would bring in.

Minus side, she was pretty sure she'd been about to kiss John again.

By all rights, she should have been relieved by the interruption.

She was relieved.

Mostly.

Smog it, she thought as the doctor waved to someone on the other side of the pub.

"Just letting my associates know I found you," Natsiq explained as he dropped into the chair John offered.

"Associates?" she asked, turning with John to spy a tall, slender figure with coppery skin and ink-black hair weaving through the crowded tables.

They were followed, Jagati noted, by someone of much shorter stature, the only visible feature being a mop of brown hair lightly touched with silver.

"Well, two of them," Dr. Natsiq explained. "Dr. Panesar is still at the airfield, inventorying our supplies. The other two came with me. My eldest, Kallik." Natsiq indicated the taller of the approaching pair with visible pride. "They are also a doctor."

"Two Dr. Natsiq's?" Jagati focused on the elder physician. "Doesn't that get confusing?"

"It would," Alain agreed, "but Kallik uses their full name, Natsiq-Corvais."

"I try to," the young doctor in question said as they arrived at the table, a goblet of red wine in hand and a twinkle in their dark eyes, "but generally our patients give up and call us Dr. A and Dr. K."

"They do not," their father replied.

"They do when you're not listening," Kallik said with an infectious grin.

The elder doctor rolled his eyes. "And this is Pyotr Aaberg," he continued as the last of the party broke through the crush, carrying two pint glasses.

Jagati, turning to the newcomer, felt a sense of shock.

Why, she couldn't say as, aside from his stature, the man was about as innocuous as they came.

Then she glanced at John just in time to see him schooling his features, and realized that it wasn't *her* shock she felt, but *his*.

Smogging empathic woo woo, she thought, and gritting her teeth, she reinforced the internal walls that Eitan—who, unlike Jagati, had a lifetime of knowing he was a sensitive—had helped her construct.

"You forgot your ale, Alain," Pyotr said in a heavy Stolich-nayan accent, pushing one of the two pints he carried across the table.

"Oh, thank you." Alain accepted the drink. "Pyotr, Kallik, may I present Captain John Pitte and . . ."

Jagati filled in the expectant pause. "Jagati O'Bannion."

"Jagati is the *Errant*'s first mate," John explained.

"A pleasure to meet you," Pyotr said, climbing into the chair next to Kallik.

"And are you a doctor as well?" John asked Pyotr.

"Not me, no," Pyotr waved John's question aside. "I am merely an administrator."

"Pyotr is far more than that," Alain said. "As the team admin, he handles all the tedious details, so we in the medical staff can focus on our work."

"Interesting," John said, then glanced at Jagati before asking, "And what work do you do, precisely?"

"Nothing illegal, I assure you," Alain began.

"Just a little insane," Kallik added.

That had both Jagati and John turning to Alain, who raised his hands as if in acceptance of the judgment. "Are either of you acquainted with the organization, Medics Beyond Borders?"

"Sure." Jagati shrugged. "We've come across MBB camps a few times over the years."

"The organization does an excellent job filling in the gaps left by the keepers, with none of the same protections the keepers enjoy while doing it," John added.

"Like I said, a little insane." Kallik raised their glass in a toast to their companions.

"Not so insane this time," Pyotr said.

"We're flying to the eastern border of Stolichnaya—in February," Kallik pointed out.

"Keepers," Jagati said, then shrugged as everyone looked at her. "Not a fan of cold weather."

Alain sighed. "Unfortunately, neither was the captain of the airship we had originally chartered."

"It wasn't the cold she objected to," Kallik said, their voice taking on an edge.

"Is that so?" John glanced at the younger doctor.

"Captain LeVeau has opinions on just who Medics Beyond Borders should be helping," Alain explained. "In that she believes we shouldn't be helping anyone outside colonial borders."

"Talk about missing the brief," Jagati muttered as, from the other side of the pub, the musicians transitioned to a louder, faster piece.

"No succor to the enemy?" John guessed, pitching his voice up to be heard over the clapping that accompanied the music.

"Never mind that there are as many MBB members in the Coalition as there are in the United Colonies," Kallik pointed out.

"Which is why we came looking for you," Pyotr added, glancing at John.

Alain nodded. "After LeVeau cancelled on our contract, we went to the airfield office, and a fellow named Alvaro mentioned the *Errant* had just returned to Nike and might suit our needs."

"We might," John said, his eyes darting to Pyotr and back to Alain. "But there are some matters to discuss, first."

"We have the fee," Alain said before naming a sum that Jagati judged as just on the right side of doable.

"Which is good to know," John replied, "but money isn't the only issue."

"Please," Kallik held up their hand, "if you're going to turn us down, do it fast so we can start looking for another airship."

"We're not turning you down," Jagati said, glancing at John.

"Not at all," he agreed. "We merely like to go into a deal with a certain amount of transparency."

"Meaning?" Pyotr asked.

"Meaning, the *Errant* is an older 'ship," Jagati explained. "Like, liquid-aluminum battery old. No crystal power."

"Oh, if that's all . . ." Alain appeared ready to wave that off.

"Not entirely," John said.

"We've also got sparse guest furnishings," Jagati said.

"And a dodgy engine pod," John added.

"Not to mention the twenty-year-old bact-system, so water rationing is a necessity," Jagati continued.

"Basically, the *Errant* isn't the fastest, or most comfortable, transport on the airfield," John concluded.

"Forgive me," Alain said, "but this still feels as if you are turning us down—just more politely."

"It's more that we like to under promise and overdeliver," John said.

"There's a reason we carry freight more often than passengers," Jagati added before picking up her drink. "It can get a little boring and a lot ripe."

"You realize we work in aid camps, don't you?" Kallik asked.

"Fair point," John admitted, then met Jagati's gaze.

She glanced at the doctors, and Pyotr, then back to John. She dipped her head, and he turned to the waiting clients.

"And it looks like we have an understanding."

"Excellent," Alain smiled. "Pyotr, you have the contract still?"

"Right here," Pyotr patted his coat while Jagati rose from her chair to wave wildly at the dance floor.

"Figure we should get Eitan in on the conversation," she explained at John's questioning glance. "Eitan's one of the crew," she said to the others. "Our mechanic already called it a night, but you'll meet him soon enough."

"Smog it to Earth and back," Pyotr swore, then looked up, sheepishly. "I seem to have dropped the contract somewhere."

"Possibly at the bar?" John asked.

"Seems most likely," Pyotr said, sliding off his chair.

"I'll—" Kallik began.

"I'll help you look for it," John cut in, popping up from his seat. "We'll be back soon," he promised.

"If you're sure," Kallik said, though they sounded perfectly happy to remain and enjoy their wine.

"We will be fine," Pyotr promised as first John, then he, turned to push through the surrounding tables.

"I hope the contract isn't on the floor," Alain said, eyeing the sticky floorboards.

"Did you say something about another crew member?" Kallik asked.

Jagati looked back at the dance floor and realized Eitan hadn't noticed her earlier hail.

"Hold on a sec," she said, jumping from the chair and heading toward the rhythmic crowd.

Halfway to her goal, she huffed out a breath and decided to try something different.

Standing still, she focused all her attention on Eitan's enthusiastically spinning figure and was rewarded by the sudden flick of his head in her direction.

As soon as their eyes met, she jerked her chin, which afforded her a quick nod from Eitan who immediately broke away from the dancers to join her.

"Possible job," she explained, leading him back to the table.

"One you seem less than pleased by," he said, reminding her he could sense more than her summons.

"The job is fine," she replied. "But there's something off about Pitte."

"You know, he has a first name," Eitan murmured, but as they had reached their table, she didn't have time to hit him.

"Eitan Fehr," she flicked a hand at her crewmate as the two docs rose from their chairs, "meet Dr. Natsiq and Dr. Natsiq-Corvais."

"Pleased to make your acquaintance," Alain said before relaxing back into his chair.

"Please, call me Kallik," the younger Natsiq inserted smoothly, reaching out their hand to grasp Eitan's.

Sweet merciful keeper's hive, she thought, as the smile Eitan gave Kallik nearly made Jagati's head swim.

"Both doctors, you say?" Eitan asked as he, Kallik, and Jagati took their seats. "Are either of you acquainted with Tiago Hama? He is a friend, about to graduate from Yousafzai Medical."

"We haven't met, but then, we both graduated from Oronhy-atekha, in Moosehead," Alain explained.

While the Natsiqs and Eitan made nice, Jagati thought about the way John had been so eager to help Pyotr find the missing contract.

Something's up, there, she thought, tapping her glass.

But what?

John remained silent as he moved through the crowded tavern, dodging the occasional swinging mug or wayward elbow as he went.

He did not stop at the bar but rather turned in the direction of the tavern's entrance and then through the door.

Stepping out onto the Rigging's sheltered porch, he took a deep breath of the chill night air before leaning against a pillar, crossing his arms, and staring out into the street. "It's been a long time," he said as the other man came up alongside him, "Pascal."

"Long enough for you to improve your poker face," the man who'd been introduced as Pyotr Aaberg said. The Stoli dialect had been replaced with something close to John's own Mooseheadian accent. "And it was already a good poker face. Civilian life looks well on you."

"Does that surprise you?" John glanced down, saw the green eyes flash with a quick hint of amusement in the light from the tavern window.

"A little," Pascal admitted, shoving his hands in his coat pockets and turning his gaze toward the rain-spattered road. "You were very keen on the Air Corps. I suppose I thought you'd be a lifer."

"I might have been," John replied. "But as you probably heard, that choice was taken away from me at Nasa."

"I did hear about that," Pascal agreed. "But not until a few years later. I was occupied . . . elsewhere."

"Of course you were," John murmured as a rickshaw came spinning down the street, spraying water everywhere

Someone inside the tavern had started singing "The Last Time I Saw Guinness" and a rush of voices joined in.

"You probably don't know this," Pascal continued, "but Special Operations opened a quiet—very quiet—investigation into Nasa soon after the event. I know one of the officers assigned, and he is nothing if not tenacious. The truth will come out."

"Some of it may already have," John replied, thinking back to his recent meeting with Gideon Quinn—another officer blind-sided by the events at Nasa.

"That's good then," Pascal said. "Still, I was sorry to hear of your part in it."

"I had no 'part' in any of the affair," John said tightly. "I was attempting to follow regulations, and I was stabbed in the back—literally—before being court martialed and my crew demoted and scattered throughout the fleet, all at the whim of the armchair general who commandeered my 'ship to commit murder."

At John's outburst, Pascal cleared his throat.

"Forgive me," John said as, with some effort, he bundled the familiar rage up like an old carpet, to be dumped back into the mental closet where it lived.

"Nothing to forgive," Pascal said evenly. "Though I believe the Air Corps owes you and your crew more than an apology."

"I'd as soon have nothing more to do with the Air Corps," John said, dragging his eyes back to Pascal's before adding, "Or any other part of the Corps, come to that."

"Ah," Pascal said. "Now we come to it."

"I don't want my 'ship, or my crew, involved in any of Special Operations' activities," John said.

"What makes you think I'm still with Special Ops?" Pascal

asked, but quietly, as a couple stepped out of the pub and, sharing an umbrella, dashed down the sidewalk in the direction of the tram stop.

John waited for the amorous pair to turn the corner before replying. "You mean, besides the fact your name isn't Pyotr Aaberg, you're not from Stolichnaya, and you've never shown the least interest in charitable works?"

"You wound me." Pascal clutched a hand to his heart. "I've given generously to several charities over the years."

"Pascal . . ."

"Fine. Yes. I am on an assignment. And no, I can't tell you what it is."

"And what about the Natsiqs?"

"Oh, they're quite real. Real doctors, really working with MBB. As is Dr. Panesar."

"Panesar? Oh, the one at the airfield," John said, recalling Alain's earlier mention of a third associate. "But tell me, do you, or General Satsuke, or anyone in Special Ops, care what will happen to the good doctors or their organization if your cover is blown?"

"Please." Pascal scoffed at that. "There is not an intelligence agency on Fortune that hasn't embedded their operatives in various and sundry rescue organizations. In fact, I can guarantee there's at least one Midasian spy working on the Fordian border, right now."

"And how many innocent doctors will be arrested by the Colonial Corps should that Midasian operative be discovered?" John asked. "How many will be interrogated?"

"Are you implying the Corps tortures their prisoners?" Pascal's question was undercut by one of the new crystal-powered autos speeding past at what had to be thirty kph.

"Did I mention I was stabbed in the back on my own bridge while a general of the Corps looked on?" John asked in return. "More to the point, we know several of the Coalition states *do* torture their prisoners. Can you say, with one-hundred percent certainty, that those three doctors on your team won't suffer if you are discovered?"

"My cover has never yet been blown," Pascal said. "But, assuming such a catastrophe were to occur, I've been assured that the rest of the team will be protected—and yes," he added as John opened his mouth to protest, "I believe it. Not that I blindly trust the brass, but I do know they aren't willing to weather the public smog storm that would erupt if something happened to a group of volunteers under our watch."

"Vague and political," John observed. "How very Spec Ops."

"Something you would know well given that even after you left Spec Ops, you continued to be one of Satsuke's operatives."

"I was nothing more than a courier," John pointed out. "Like almost every fleet captain out there."

"You were more than that. I read the report on that Midasian cell you uncovered in Dodge. And the exfil in Isroa."

"And look where all that got me."

Pascal sighed, looked up. "Stabbed in the back?"

"Exactly."

"That won't happen this time," Pascal said.

"You can't know that."

"Perhaps not, but I do know that the northern refugees truly need aid. It's just your bad luck that the *Errant* is the only available transport. So the only question remaining is if your resentment of all things Special Operations is great enough to prevent civilians on both sides of the border from receiving food, shelter, and medical care?"

Both men fell silent as the tavern door opened again, this time to an aeronaut who paused, blinked owlishly at the rain before shrugging, clomping down the short steps, and splashing her way in the direction of the airfield.

"John?"

He turned back to see Pascal's gaze—open, earnest, and as innocent as a murder hornet. "Fine. We'll take the job."

"Thank you."

"Just see we get paid," John said as he straightened. "And don't include my name in your reports."

"You have my word."

"For what that's worth," John muttered as the other man produced the "missing" contract from his inner pocket. "But before we rejoin the others, you should know that keeping your secret from the crew won't be easy."

"I think you forget how good I am," Pascal said, leading the way back into the pub.

"And humble," John pointed out, following the other man into the wall of heat and noise. He leaned down so Pascal could hear him. "But what I mean is, two of my crew are sensitives."

At that, Pascal came to a halt. "You couldn't have mentioned that at the start?"

With the barest hint of a smile, John patted him on the shoulder. "I imagine you'll be fine if you avoid Jagati—and whatever you do, do not let Eitan seduce you."

"Please. I'm a professional," Pascal scoffed, once again using Pyotr Aaberg's Stolichnayan accent.

And then they reached the table where the rest of their party was waiting.

Which was when Pascal set eyes on Eitan Fehr for the first time. "Why, this is hell," he muttered.

"*Professional*," John reminded him, sotto voce, before announcing, "We found the contract."

CHAPTER 2

RORY MCCABE, WHO WAS DEEP INSIDE THE AFT PORT engine pod when John and Jagati returned to the *Errant*, wasn't surprised to learn that Eitan hadn't made it back to the 'ship, but he was surprised the crew already had a new job booked.

"We'll be lifting off at fourteen hundred," John explained while Rory continued to clean a corroded battery port.

"Late start," Rory commented, blinking against the smell of the cleaning fluid.

"It'll take that long to get the cargo loaded," John explained from where he crouched outside the pod. "But that also gives us time to make certain Jinna has a safe place to stay."

"About that," Rory glanced at his captain, then reached for the almost-new power pack he meant to affix to the pod's now clean battery ports. "Turns out we had a telgram from Gideon Quinn waiting when we returned to the 'ship."

John, who Rory knew shared an uncomfortable history with Quinn, leaned forward. "Did he have any further news?"

"Only repeated that Jinna would be safe in Nike, and offered to stand her to a room at the Hotel Elysium, with Mia, for as long as she needed."

"Mia will be pleased, I'm sure," John noted with a smile.

"Jinna was," Rory admitted as he focused on the power pack, a task that was almost demanding enough to distract him from the fact that Jinna would be leaving the *Errant*, almost on the heels of having learned she reciprocated his feelings.

Still, he reminded himself, they'd have the morning. And it would ease his mind, at least a little, to see Jinna was well settled before they lifted off.

"Speaking of Jinna . . ." now Jagati poked her head through the pod's hatch, angling to peer around John. "Why are you in here mucking with an old engine instead of snuggled in bed with the new girlfriend?"

"Jagati," John warned.

"Like you weren't wondering." Jagati poked him in the shoulder before glaring at Rory. "So? What gives?"

Rory grimaced but knew Jagati was not one to let up.

"I'm in here," he told her, "because, for one, we need all our engines functioning to be able to fly, and for another, I'd imagine no one here has tried to share an airship-sized bed with an expectant mum?"

"Can't say as I have," John admitted.

"Nope," Jagati agreed.

"Didn't think so," Rory muttered.

"That said," John continued, "you'd best not stay up too late. Between getting Jinna situated at the Elysium, load-in, and pre-flight, tomorrow will be a busy day."

"I vote we make Eitan clear the bact-tanks," Jagati suggested, referring to the fixtures responsible for recycling the 'ship's waste and gray water. Located on the lowest deck of the gondola, the bact-tanks provided both filtration and ballast.

They were also, Rory well knew, as pungent as a compost heap and thrice as dangerous. All of which meant no one enjoyed policing them for clogs, leaks—or, worst of all—a failure of the bacteria to thrive. "I second that vote," he said, adding the grin he knew his crewmates were looking for.

He didn't know how successful the smile was, but after a beat, John shooed Jagati back, and they left Rory to finish his work.

When the engine pod was as flight ready as he could make it, Rory was still too wound up to sleep, so he climbed up to the galley to read for a spell.

He was well into his novel—one of a box of dreadfuls John had found in the bargain bin outside a Nike bookstore—when Eitan entered the galley.

"Care for some tea?" Eitan asked, moving to the stove.

"Wouldn't argue," Rory replied and, over the edge of the book, watched his one-handed crewmate fill the kettle and set it on the galley's flameless heating unit. "You're on rota for the pre-flight bact-tank check."

"Maybe I should make this a bottle of wine, instead," Eitan said, though he continued with his preparations, heating the pot and adding three scoops of tea to it while the water heated.

Rory noted Eitan had chosen chamomile—in deference to the late hour, he supposed—and, once the kettle began to shriek, poured the steaming water into the pot.

He carried the pot to the table, fetched mugs and strainer, and poured out.

All with just the one hand.

"Thanks," Rory said, setting down the book.

"My pleasure."

In unison, each man raised their mug, blew at the steam, and took a cautious sip.

The floral scent wreathed the air as Rory lowered his mug. "You're home sooner than I expected," he said before he thought better of it.

"And you are not in your cabin with Jinna, as I might have expected," Eitan observed.

"Narrow bed, pregnant woman," Rory pointed out.

"Of course," Eitan murmured, taking another sip.

"Only," Rory continued on his original track, "I can't help but notice you're always back sooner than I'd have expected. That is to say, you never spend the night."

"I haven't noticed any of the others, yourself included, staying anywhere but the *Errant*."

"And if any one of us received even a third of the offers you do, you could put hard starbucks on it that we would be sleeping elsewhere." Even as he said this, Rory thought how, now that he and Jinna were—well—he and Jinna, he might indeed find himself sleeping somewhere else . . . from time to time.

"You keep a count?" Eitan asked, drawing Rory's attention.

"No." Rory picked up his mug. Put it down. Picked it up again. "Maybe."

Eitan's lips turned up in a hint of a smile, and both men took another sip of tea, sighed, and set their mugs down with a gentle double-*thump*.

Rory glanced at his book, then up at Eitan, who was watching him.

"You may ask," Eitan said.

Rory frowned. "I thought you only sensed another body's thoughts on physical contact."

"Usually true, but . . ." this time Eitan paused, shook his head. "I can see the curiosity written on your face. You have a question. Ask."

"Fine then." Rory leaned over his tea to meet the other man's dark gaze. "Why don't you spend the night with any of your lovers? Or bring them here? Ever?"

Despite having prompted the question, Eitan let out a soft breath before responding, "I have bad dreams."

"Bad dreams?" Rory echoed. "But doesn't everyone? I mean," he continued, waving a hand, "Keepers, after near to twenty years of war, I'd be more surprised if a body *didn't* have nightmares. Which I suppose you'd know, what with being a sensitive and all, and . . ."

And here Rory's voice faltered as he recalled that, yes, Eitan was a sensitive and, as previously noted, one who—on physical contact—could feel what another felt as well as share their thoughts.

It was, Rory supposed, a part of what made him such a popular bedmate, as who wouldn't want a lover who could sense their needs, their pleasures . . . and share his own?

But what if the sharing didn't stop when the lovemaking ended?

I have bad dreams.

Eitan, a veteran of the war and a survivor of years in the Adian arenas, would have no shortage of fuel for his nightmares.

Rory blinked, then focused on the other man, who was watching him, patiently waiting for the quarterstar to drop.

"No off toggle," Rory murmured, meeting Eitan's patient gaze. "You're still a sensitive, even in your sleep." He paused, then recalled another conversation, directly after Eitan had joined the crew, when Rory was a little drunk and a lot lonely. "Is that why you turned me down that one time?"

Eitan's head dipped in a nod as he set his mug down. "There was a time . . . before the war, before Adia, I could spend the night in a lover's arms. Only once did my dreams travel, and that was with another sensitive." Here he paused, and a shadow seemed to pass over his expression, but then he shook his head before resting his left arm—the one missing a hand—on the table. "That has changed," he said simply. "And while it may be the height of rudeness to slip from a lover's bed so soon after the gift of sharing, of the two offenses," he glanced down at the hand that wasn't there, then up at Rory, "it seems to me that walking away is the lesser."

"I suppose it would be," Rory murmured as the truth struck home.

The truth that, no matter how close Eitan became to another, at the end of the night, he would always be alone.

Eitan, meanwhile, gave a simple nod before downing the rest of his tea. Rising, he put the cup in the sink for Jagati to complain about in the morning, then strode out of the galley.

But just as Rory was picking up his book, Eitan turned, started to say something, then stopped.

Rory set the book down. "You have a question of your own?" he guessed.

"After a fashion. I just wondered . . . we have been working together for many months, yet not a one of the crew has asked about this." He held up his left arm. "As far as I can sense, no one wants to."

"Ah, well." Rory picked up his book again. "We on the *Errant* tend to live by the Air Corps motto, don't we?"

"I was Infantry," Eitan reminded him. "I have never heard the Air Corps motto."

"Well, then, to further your education . . . ." Rory raised his mug, as if in a toast. "'Leave your past on the ground, lest it weigh you down,'" he quoted, then drank.

"Interesting," Eitan said as Rory lowered his mug. "Someday, perhaps, you can teach me how to do that."

With that statement, he left Rory with his tea, his book, and a strange twisting in his chest.

The rising of Fortune's two suns saw Eitan in the lower depths of the *Errant*'s gondola, wearing a full-face mask as he scanned the workings of the bact-tanks.

He discovered and dealt with a clog in one of the intake pipes, then added more charcoal to the filters, as well as a few handfuls of dried algae to provide a balanced diet for what Rory referred to as the "wee bacterium."

Once assured the tanks themselves were in as good a shape as could be hoped at their advanced age, he doffed the mask and climbed straight to his quarters to clean up before heading back down to the cargo bay, where John was already lowering the aft ramp.

He shook back his damp hair and joined Rory and Jagati. "Jinna is settled?" he asked Rory, who appeared more than a little forlorn.

"Moved into a room at a very nice Keeper's hotel," Rory said. "She was setting down to tea with Mia and about a half-dozen other dodgers, or, former dodgers I should say, as I was leaving. Bact tanks sorted?" he asked in his turn.

Eitan nodded. "I fed the bacteria, topped up the charcoal, and there was one clog, taken care of. Also, I used everyone's shower rations."

Rory shared a glance with Jagati. "All's fair in love and sewage," he determined.

"Happy to give to the cause," Jagati agreed as they heard the dull rumble of an approaching crawler. "Doctors are prompt," she added, slapping both the men on their shoulders before tromping across the deck where John was already striding down the ramp.

Rory unhitched the dolly, and he and Eitan both followed their crewmates outside, where the damp tarmac was steaming in the chill sunslight.

Here they met the two doctors Natsiq and Pyotr, as well as Dr. Lakshmay Panesar, a woman of middle years with a reassuringly stout figure and a pronounced limp.

Given their flight window, there wasn't much time for extended introductions.

Doctors Natsiq and Panesar unloaded the crawler while Pyotr tallied every item in his notebook before the rest of the party hauled the cargo into the airship, where it was secured for flight.

With everyone working together, the cargo was loaded with plenty of time for Eitan to return the crawler to the airfield's mech bay.

By the time he arrived back at the *Errant*, the cargo bay was deserted but for Dr. Panesar, who Eitan found perched on one of the secured crates, holding a tiny screwdriver and what looked to be a sinuous metal sculpture of a leg, a booted foot dangling loosely from the ankle.

Coming to a halt, he looked down and saw her left foot braced on the floor and her right trouser leg rolled up to show a cloth-covered stump just below her knee.

He looked up as she did. "I apologize," he said, clearing his throat and looking at the water casks locked down in the middle of the deck. "I didn't mean to intrude."

"Hardly an intrusion." The doctor waived her screwdriver as if to dismiss the thought. "Just having some issues with one of the joints." She turned back to the leg in her hand as she added, "Doesn't bother me if it doesn't bother you."

Eitan frowned, but looking back at the woman he could see—and sense—that she spoke the truth.

Then he looked more closely at the prosthetic itself and stepped forward despite himself. "I've never seen a limb of that design. It seems so—insubstantial."

"Allusteel." She tapped the screwdriver on the "tibia," which made a satisfying *ting*. "Strong enough for whatever situation we encounter on the job and light enough for . . . whatever situation we encounter on the job that I have to run away from."

He glanced up, saw the twinkle in her brown eyes, and felt the tug of a smile. Then he looked down again, taking in the almost fluid bend of the allusteel into the boot, which she was removing now. "Does it—" he began, then stopped and looked into her eyes. Seeing nothing but quiet acceptance, he continued. "Does it hurt?"

"The stump does," she admitted, setting the boot aside before applying the screwdriver to a connection in the ankle. "When I first put it on, and after a long day." She looked up. "But much as it hurts, it doesn't pain me as much as not losing it would have. It was a case of lose the limb or lose my life." She shrugged, removed the screw, which was stripped, Eitan now saw, and pulled another out of the tool pouch at her side. "I'd say it was a good trade. Though I still get enough shots of the phantom pain to make up for the lack of bunions."

"For me, the problem is less the phantom pain than the ghost of the limb itself," Eitan admitted. "The way I keep reaching for things, or trying to lean on something—" For a wonder, he felt himself flush. "Not so much as when I first lost it, but sometimes . . ."

"I cannot tell you how many times I wake up in the morning, swing my 'legs' out of bed, and land on my butt because I not only forgot I'd lost it, but swore I could *feel* it there."

"How long ago did you lose it?"

"Three years and some change," she said, setting the screwdriver aside and testing the joint. "Took about a year to adjust to walking with Nan here—"

"Nan?" Eitan started. "You *named* it?"

"Of course." She grinned as she tucked away the driver and reached for the boot. "She's part of me, and I need her support, but she's not *of* me, so why not give her a name?"

Eitan glanced down at his left arm, where the spring blade Rory had made him was buckled securely under the abbreviated sleeve.

He wondered what name would suit the device, then wondered if naming any of the other prosthetics Rory had constructed would have made them more palatable.

Unlikely, he thought, looking up to see Dr. Panesar, with practiced ease, settling the leg over the sock on her knee. "How did it happen?" he began, then added, "If I may ask?"

"Our crawler hit an IED, in Midas," she replied easily, before looking up. "You?"

He glanced at his arm and hesitated only a second before pulling up the sleeve and angling his arm for her to see the stump under the spring-blade over his forearm. "Sword," he said shortly, "in western Adia."

"Ouch." She studied the arm a moment. "Where did the burns come from?" She nodded at the scarring running up his arm.

"I had to cauterize the injury. There was little time for finesse, in the moment."

Which, Eitan determined, was more than enough sharing for one day, so he rolled down his sleeve while the doctor rolled down her trouser leg.

"Do you need assistance with the stairs?" he asked, holding out his hand and, when she took it added, "or. . . anything else?"

She looked up, and he saw when she understood what else he was offering.

Her eyes widened, and she shook her head with amusement. "Thank you, Msr Fehr, but I think not." Then she added an infectious grin. "Maybe if I were a little younger . . ."

Eitan shook his own head. "You are the perfect age for yourself."

"And you are very smooth," she countered. "But I think, should I accept, the bed might be a bit crowded."

Eitan blinked. "Crowded?"

"You know, between you . . . me . . . your ghost arm . . . my ghost leg . . ."

"Our mattresses are a bit small." Eitan accepted the deflection with a grin of his own, then watched as she made her way to the ladder and, true to her word, ascended the stairs with only the hint of a limp.

Alone, he crossed back to close the ramp, and as it creaked into place, he thought of phantom limbs which led, inevitably, to thoughts of other ghosts.

Alexi, Margot, Vikram, Conn, Jaime, Branson . . . and all the other Adian prisoners whose names he hadn't had a chance to learn because . . .

Well . . . because.

Then the ramp thudded into place, and Eitan spun the lock closed and left the cargo bay behind.

But the ghosts, as always, followed.

CHAPTER 3

JAGATI FELT RATHER SMUG AS SHE STIRRED THE RED-brown mass in the pot. Admittedly, it didn't look like much, but it smelled great, which was a first for Jagati.

In fact, it was because her cooking had become a running joke aboard the *Errant* that Jagati had asked Jinna Pride—who was not only the love of Rory's life, but an actual professional in the kitchen—what she could prepare that would not require a lot of attention.

Or effort.

Or skill.

"Deus Ex Masala," had been Jinna's immediate response, then patiently waited for Jagati's guffaws to end before describing what Jagati needed to dump into a single giant pot and occasionally stir.

Since it sounded like something she could actually manage—possibly that was the Deus Ex part of it—Jagati had, for once, been looking forward to her assigned dinner shift, a full three days after departing from Nike.

Giving the bubbling masala another stir, she figured it would be worth the wait, especially after Rory's snarky comment on how lucky they were that the passengers were doctors and could likely handle a case of food poisoning.

And right after *that* observation, John had offered to take over her galley shift.

Well, smog that, she thought, turning to poke at the pot of rice to discover it was a bit scorched on the bottom, but she liked the added crunch.

Shutting off the heat under the rice, she took a satisfied whiff of the stew which, okay, singed the inside of her nostrils, but the *Errant* crew liked a little heat.

Hopefully the doctors would too.

And Pyotr, the not-a-doc.

Thinking of Pyotr, Jagati let out a speculative *hmmm*.

Despite the original shock she'd sensed from John the night they'd met Pyotr, she hadn't caught even a hint of unease since the Stolichnayan had come aboard.

Then again, the two men hadn't crossed paths in Jagati's presence since liftoff.

In fact, as far as she could tell, Pyotr only emerged from his cabin at dinner, and John had taken helm duty during the dinner shift for the duration of the trip.

And speaking of dinner . . . she grabbed a tasting spoon and scooped out a sample. "Yup, that is some heat," she said aloud before tossing the spoon into the sink, where it clattered against the pile of measuring cups, spoons, and empty tins.

Good thing it was Rory's night to clean up.

"What is yon smell?"

Speak of the poacher, Jagati thought. "Dinner," she said, covering the pot as Rory himself swung into the galley, all gangly limbs and curiosity.

"That can't be right," Rory said, his brow furrowing as he aimed for the stove. "It smells . . . good."

"Are you saying that nothing I make ever tastes good?"

"Can ye argue with me?"

She couldn't quite contain the snort of laughter as she conceded his point. "I may have gotten tired of stinking at this and asked Jinna for some suggestions."

As always, at the mention of Jinna's name, Rory lit up like a nova. But this time, the light dimmed faster than a desert sunsset.

"What is it?" Jagati asked, grabbing the wooden spoon and using it as a pointer. "Don't tell me there's trouble in paradise. You and Jinna have been an item for what, a week? What could go wrong in eight days?"

"There's no trouble," he said, reaching past her to lift the lid on the pot, then yanking his hand back when Jagati swept the spoon down in a chopping motion.

"Oy! Tetchy much?" Rory asked.

"Avoiding much?" she challenged.

He glared.

She raised an eyebrow.

"Fine." He raised his hands in surrender. "It's nae a problem with Jinna. It's just . . . I just . . ."

"You don't like leaving her." Jagati filled the uncertain pause before she could stop herself.

Rory's eyes widened, and Jagati was pretty sure hers had too.

"I swear, I wasn't trying to read you," she said quickly, waving both hands, including the one with the spoon which shot a rain of masala down on Rory. "Oops."

"Ha," he said before a quick grin flashed, and he brushed at the splattered sauce, opting to taste the ammunition. "Keepers," he said, his brows shooting up. "I can't say what's more impressive—that you've made something tasty, or this new sensitivity you've got happening."

"Ha." she echoed his sentiment but couldn't stop the hunch of her shoulders as she turned back to the stove where, smog it, there was nothing left to do.

"Here." She spun and shoved Rory in the direction of the cabinets. "You can set the table."

"Since when are you the boss of me?" he groused.

"I'm the first mate," she reminded him. "Which means I'm always the boss of you."

As she spoke, two of their four passengers appeared in the galley's starboard entrance.

"Dr. Panesar, Dr. A—I mean, Natsiq," Jagati greeted the physicians as both the tall, lean Natsiq and the short, solid Panesar visibly sniffed the air with anticipation.

"I really don't mind the nickname," the elder Natsiq said. "I just like Kallik to think I do."

"And I believe we can dispense with all the titles for now," Dr. Panesar said, her gold nose ring glinting in the overhead lamps as she limped over to observe Jagati's labors. "At least until we need to impress someone."

Jagati grinned at the other woman who, to her mind, didn't need a title to impress anyone.

Less because of the loss of her leg in action than because, when Lakshmay Panesar walked into a room, compassion followed.

So far, Jagati had met only one other individual with the same capacity for just plain *caring* that Lakshmay embodied.

She didn't know if it was a curse or a blessing that said *other individual* was also her captain and business partner—and the most decent, solid, honest-to-a-fault man she'd ever known.

All of which was fine. It was good.

A person should be able to trust their captain and business partner.

But then there'd been that moment in the cargo bay, permanently altering the playing field. And later, at the pub, when John had left the metaphorical ball in Jagati's net, allowing her to decide if she meant to try for a goal or retire from said field.

Not that she'd be suiting up for a game while they had a 'ship full of passengers, she reminded herself, tuning back into the chatter as Alain and Rory set the table.

At her side, Lakshmay dug the pitcher of hyacinth tea they kept stocked from the cooler and grabbed a stack of mugs, taking everything to the table.

Jagati picked up the stew and, following Lakshmay, set the pot on its trivet.

. . . and thought of John, alone, up on the bridge.

Maybe she could bring his dinner to him and take the helm while he ate.

And as he ate, they could talk—talking wasn't suiting up—in relative privacy.

At least, until Eitan arrived for his shift at the helm.

And then what? she asked herself.

And then, her mind wound around as she fetched the rice, *maybe we could head to John's quarters and talk some more.*

After all, talking had never been a problem with them. In fact, John was one of the few humans Jagati enjoyed sharing a conversation with.

And maybe, after they'd conversed a while—

"What smells so good?" Kallik asked, striding into the galley.

"Ah . . ." Jagati blinked and shook off the sense memory of John's cedar-scented soap. "It's—"

"Chana Masala, if I'm not mistaken," Lakshmay said, taking the lid off the pot and peering inside.

"Got it in one," Jagati said. *Thank Deus Ex.*

"I notice you didn't slap at Lakshmay for peeking," Rory pointed out from the other side of the table.

"That's because Lakshmay is a guest," Jagati told him with a sisterly sneer. "And it's ready to eat," she added as Eitan, who was always on time for a meal, arrived.

"Dinner smells wonderful," he said, which didn't necessarily signify, as Eitan tended to eat anything that was put in front of him.

"Jinna's recipe," Jagati said.

"Jinna?" Kallik asked.

"Rory's *delbar-am*," Eitan explained.

"Awww," Kallik said, beaming.

"Aye, all right, then." Rory, flushed at the mention of his beloved, tossed some napkins in Kallik's direction, but they caught the pile of linens with a grin and joined in the communal table prep.

Jagati, grabbing the nearest bowl to begin serving, barely suppressed her own grin.

"Where's Pyotr?" Alain asked as he scraped a chair back from the table.

"With John on the bridge," Eitan said as he—ever the risto—pulled out a chair for Lakshmay, then Kallik, both of whom flushed.

Jagati, ladling masala over rice, paused at that because, while passengers weren't precisely unwelcome on the bridge, visits without an invitation were discouraged.

Lakshmay, however, nodded as she took the bowl from Jagati before passing it along to Kallik who passed it to Alain. "Captain Pitte said we may be running into some weather, so Pyotr wanted to radio the Kopernik camp, and let them know of possible delays."

"Huh. Maybe I should take them both a tray," Jagati said before she could think.

But when she did think, it occurred to her that a chance to get a read on John and Pyotr together would be almost as rewarding as . . . as exploring the borders of the idea of suiting up.

Rory's snort, however, had her looking up. "What?"

"Just wondering when you were demoted to yeoman," Rory said.

"Oh, sting." Jagati rolled her eyes. "But seriously, I don't want to risk John not getting some of this meal and then not believing it was edible."

Even as she spoke, she spied Alain looking up from his bowl with an alarmed expression.

"I mean, more edible than my usual," she said, but that didn't sound much better.

"I'm sure it is more than edible," Lakshmay said, taking her own bowl from Jagati's hand and immediately digging in her spoon to take a heaping bite.

Everyone at the table, Jagati included, froze.

Lakshmay's eyes crinkled as she swallowed and smiled. "Much more than edible," she said. "It is delicious. Just the right touch of coriander," she added as Jagati resisted—barely—the urge to cheer.

"Well, then, it appears you must take John and Pyotr a tray," Eitan said as Jagati handed him a bowl.

"Take a tray where?" Pyotr asked, appearing in the starboard door.

"To the bridge, for you and the captain," Kallik told him.

"No one wanted you to miss this wonderful dinner," Lakshmay added with a wink at Jagati.

"A kind thought," Pyotr said with an absent wave. "But unfortunately, Captain Pitte sent me to tell you a fast-moving storm has risen between Kopernik and our location."

"Stolichnaya in February," Alain said with a sigh, at the same moment the airship gave a sudden, wicked jerk.

Only years of flight kept Jagati from dropping the bowl in her hand as the 'ship's klaxon sounded three long tones.

"Storm," Rory, Jagati, and Pyotr all said at once, each holding down whatever items on the table were closest.

"All hands to emergency stations," John's voice came from the 'ship's speakers. "Passengers, anything that's not locked down, get it locked down. This may be a bumpy ride."

Wasting no time on curses—though she had a few dozen to spare— Jagati dumped all the untouched stew back in the pot, replaced the lid, and hauled the pot into the cooler while standing aside for Rory to put in the rice pot and Lakshmay to shove the pitcher of tea into its slot.

"Dishes here." Eitan yanked a deep tub from under one of the counters.

"Then back to your berths," Jagati ordered. "And don't forget to stow anything you don't want flying into your face."

"Ouch," said Kallik, but all the passengers did as they were told.

With the galley secured, Eitan headed down-ladder to confirm the cargo was likewise safely stowed, and Rory and Jagati raced up-ladder to tend to the envelope and assist John at the helm, respectively.

As another gust knocked the gondola sideways. Jagati caught the ladder rail and, this time, let the curses fly.

Not only had she lost the chance to suss out the tension between John and Pyotr—or between John and herself, for that matter—she'd finally made a decent dinner, and now it looked like no one was going to get a chance to eat it.

CHAPTER 4

THE STORM PROVED SO INTENSE JOHN WAS FORCED TO land the *Errant* in the closest airfield, just outside the Stolichnayan city of Upsilon.

They were still at anchor the following afternoon when John looked up from the chart he was rolling to see Eitan entering the bridge.

Eitan paused upon spying John. "What are you doing?"

"I thought I'd tidy the place up a bit." He held up the chart as proof. "Since we're grounded for the next day or so, it seemed as good a time as any for some housekeeping."

Both men turned to the helm, where wind-driven snow pattered against the screens.

"Winter in Stolichnaya," Eitan said, turning back to John. "You'd think we'd have learned our lesson after being grounded last year."

"At least the Upsilon airfield waived their moorage fee."

"Pyotr and Lakshmay made a strong case," Eitan said with the hint of a smile.

"I almost didn't recognize the good constable bad constable

ploy," John agreed, shooting the rolled-up map into its pigeon-hole before pulling another loose chart from under the nav table. "Speaking of our passengers, how are they doing with the delay?"

"Well enough." Eitan shrugged. "I just passed the galley, and it appears Lakshmay and Kallik are playing cards with Rory."

John looked up from the chart. "Rory cheats."

"Having just watched Lakshmay play a hand, I suspect Rory may find he's not the only one capable of bending the rules."

"Is that so?" John smiled at that. "I may head to the galley for a cup of tea once these charts are sorted." He slid the latest map into place, then grabbed the nav table as the *Errant* shuddered, rocked, and shuddered again.

Once the 'ship settled, John glanced to where Eitan had anchored himself against the weapons locker. "What brings you up to the bridge, anyway?"

"I wanted to see if there'd been any news from Gideon," he said, crossing to the telgram machine.

The mention of Gideon Quinn had John looking up from a chart detailing the topography of Allianza.

The last news they'd had from Gideon had been the telgram Rory reported the night before lift-off, offering Jinna shelter. The second-to-last had been a radio communication, during which Gideon reported that he'd solved the Nasa mystery, details to follow.

Since the events at Nasa had led to Eitan fighting for his life in the Domino arena, John could understand the other man's interest. "It's possible Gideon doesn't trust his news to the telgram operators," he pointed out, just as the telgram machine hummed to life. "But I've been known to be wrong."

Curious, he slid the Allianza chart home and joined Eitan at the comm station as the rhythmic clack of the internal keys began.

"You're not wrong this time," Eitan observed, holding up the end of the tape spitting from the machine. "The message is not from Gideon."

"And not addressed to us," John added, angling his head to read the addressee as one Pyotr Aaberg, care of the *CAS Errant*.

"I can deliver the message," Eitan offered, bracing himself as the 'ship gave another shuddering jerk.

"That's all right," John said while the telgram clacked out the end of the message, indicating no reply required. "I'll take it to him. He's probably holed up in his quarters doing paperwork." He tore the tape free, then glanced at Eitan, still staring at the now-quiet machine. "You could send a telgram to Gideon," John suggested. "Ask for generalities, at least."

"It can wait." Eitan's shoulder lifted with a hint of a shrug. "You're likely on the starbuck about his reasons. Even if Gideon were willing, I doubt the Corps would enjoy their pollution being shared over the airwaves." He paused, looked out the window, then back at John. "Perhaps I will go see how that card game is going."

"And spend some time with Kallik?"

"They are quite engaging," Eitan observed as he and John headed aft but said no more, leaving John with no idea if Eitan and Kallik had taken their flirtations any further.

And it wasn't any of his business, anyway, John reminded himself as they clattered down-ladder to the cabin deck, where Eitan waved and continued down to the common rooms.

Alone in the passage, John waited for Eitan's steps to recede before heading toward the cabin assigned to Pyotr Aaberg, accompanied only by the slivers of his shadow splitting between the soft glow of the passage lights.

As far as he could tell, Pascal had managed to avoid spending too much time with either Eitan or Jagati, and John wanted to continue that trend, if only to prevent the crew learning of his own history with Spec Ops.

Not that Eitan or Jagati would deliberately pry into Pascal's psyche; but as Eitan had confessed recently, even the most polite sensitive could pick up ripples of secrets.

Better safe, John thought, coming to a halt in front of Pascal's door at the same time a clatter of boots on allusteel had him spinning aft.

"*Whyyyy . . .*" the drawn-out word preceded the sight of Jagati, jogging up the ladderwell and into the passage, wrapped in a thick blanket that belonged to Rory.

"Why what?" John asked, flattening himself against the wall as she plowed forward.

"Why would anyone live here?" Jagati's question bounced off the walls as she tugged the blanket over her head and pounded up the passage, where she angled to port and, from the ensuing clanks, continued to race up to the bridge.

"I see she wasn't joking about not liking the cold," a Stoli-accented voice observed.

John spun on his heels, and Pascal quickly stepped back into his room, hands held out. "Sorry. No knives. I promise."

"Really?" John asked.

"None in my hands," Pascal amended.

"That sounds about right." Both men looked up, to where the sound of boots clomping on the deck above thudded forward. "But no," he added, "Jagati was not joking about the cold." He turned back to Pascal, who had lowered his hands and was still staring in the direction of the aft ladderwell. "You have a telgram," he said, holding up the tape.

"From the Kopernik camp?" Pascal asked as John handed over the tape.

"From your Uncle Alexei."

Pascal glanced up. "Did you read it?"

"That would have been intrusive," John said, then admitted, "And I assumed the message would be coded, given we both know you don't have an Uncle Alexei."

"Right," Pascal said, and began to read the message.

While he did, John peered into the other man's cabin to see the desk covered with maps, the bed strewn with ledgers.

"It's not coded," Pascal said, pulling John's attention back and handing the tape over.

John took the telgram. "'—received word from an old friend in Upsilon'," he read aloud. "'You can find Soshi playing drums at the ice tavern'." He paused, looked up. "Ice tavern? Is that a thing?"

"Apparently." Pascal reclaimed the tape. "This is my first time in Upsilon."

"I see. And do you, in fact, have an old friend named Soshi?"

At that Pascal grinned. "That I won't know until I see her. Could be any of a number of colleagues." He shot a glance down the passage before adding, "Likely Soshi, whoever she is, has some fresh intel to deliver."

"Why couldn't she just radio any intel to your—uncle?" John asked, but quietly. "If she can get a message routed to a grounded airship—"

"Too risky, this close to the Isroan border." Pascal waved that off. "Their Sig-Intel is straight out of the Midasian playbook." He sighed, looked at the tape, again. "It seems I'm going out to visit an ice tavern."

"Out?" John echoed. "As in, out, out?" He gestured vaguely as the *Errant* shifted on its anchors. "In this?"

"It's not that bad," Pascal said.

"I hate this!" The complaint echoed through the forward ladderwell, followed by the clump of boots.

"Jagati would disagree," John said, leaning against the bulkhead to make room for his frigid first mate, who came to a hopping stop as she reached the middle of the deck.

"How long until we can leave?" she asked, glaring at John, as if the weather were his fault.

"Upsilon Flight and our sonar agree the storm should move

on by tomorrow," he said, opting not to mention that, should the storm decide to move northeast, there would be no point raising anchor until it cleared Kopernik.

"Tomorrow?" she yelped. "I'm halfway to a Jagcicle *now*!" It was not clear whether the rapid stomp of her boots was an attempt to keep warm or a toddleresque tantrum.

"What's the problem?" All three turned to see Alain had appeared in the door of his quarters, a book in hand.

"Jagati was bemoaning the weather," John said.

"Understandable." Alain grimaced and clutched at the doorsill as the deck jerked beneath them.

"I've never heard tell of wild cards in Turing Twist," Rory complained, appearing in the forward ladderwell.

"That's because you've never played in Moosehead," Lakshmay's voice emerged before she appeared in Rory's wake. She blinked at the crowd in the passageway. "Are we having a party?"

"And no one invited us?" Rory added.

John cast his gaze to the ceiling and heard what might have been the leading edge of a laugh from Jagati. He met her eyes and saw a familiar glint of humor.

Passengers, she mouthed with a *what can you do?* shrug so familiar, so uniquely *her*, that John felt the gesture echo across the years, sending a ripple through the deep well of longing he'd held so close and so quiet—until that kiss in the cargo bay.

"John was bringing me a telgram from my Uncle Alexei," Pascal explained, waving the message tape. "He has news of an old friend who has settled in Upsilon."

"Why would anyone settle in Upsilon?" This, of course, from Jagati.

"I think she was following her lover," Pascal said.

"No piece is that hot," Jagati muttered.

"I would have to ask her," Pascal said with a grin. "But my uncle writes that she can be found playing drums at the Upsilon ice tavern, and I should go and see her."

"Go where?" Eitan asked.

John turned aft to see Eitan and Kallik approaching.

"Why is everyone standing in the hall?" Kallik asked.

"Passage," Lakshmay reminded them.

"Right. Why is everyone standing in the passage?" they amended.

"Well, it is warmer in a crowd," Jagati noted.

Pascal made a little sound that had John looking down to see the expression of one seeking patience.

Having felt the exact same way quite often, John almost felt sorry for him.

Almost.

"Pyotr's uncle sent word of an old friend of Pyotr's who lost her mind and moved to Upsilon," Jagati explained. "And said friend plays the drums at an ice tavern." She paused, looked at Pascal. "What fresh hell is an ice tavern, anyway?"

Pascal shrugged. "Only one way to find out." He folded the tape into his pocket. "I will need to get my coat."

"You're going out?" Kallik asked, then grinned. "Can I come with?"

"Are you all *insane?*" Jagati waved a hand and bopped John in the head.

"Ouch."

"Sorry."

"It could be interesting," Eitan said.

"I think I'll remain on the *Errant*," Alain determined as the wind buffeted the 'ship once more.

"Same here," Lakshmay agreed, tapping her leg. "Kopernik is soon enough to be dealing with the snow."

"Fair enough," Rory said. "But I admit, I'm a mite curious as to what this ice tavern might be." He glanced at John.

"Fine," John said, resigned. "Let's make a group outing of it." In part because the ice tavern sounded interesting, but mostly because the idea of his crew accompanying Pascal, ignorant of his actual purpose, didn't sit well.

"You all do what you want," Jagati said, hauling the blanket close. "There's no way on Fortune I'm going out there in this weather."

CHAPTER 5

"I can't believe you guys talked me into this," Jagati grumbled, glaring over the glittering tavern.

John and Pyotr had disappeared the moment they arrived, leaving Jagati, Eitan, Rory, and Kallik to make their way to the bar, where Eitan had stayed long enough to order a drink before sliding into the crowded pub on his own.

And the place *was* crowded, Jagati mused, despite the fact that the wind was still whipping violently enough to knock a person off her feet—and would have, had John not blocked Jagati just before her butt hit the path.

Eitan had similarly kept the rail-thin Rory from being blown into one of the massive Stolichnayan unicorns— the great, horned elasmotheres—tethered outside the tavern, while Kallik and Pyotr had both managed the trek with little difficulty.

Then again, Kallik and John were both from Moosehead, and Pyotr, from his accent at least, was a native of Stolichnaya. For them, the numbing cold and bitter storms were just weather rather than the curse against humanity Jagati knew them to be.

The locals must have a similar view to John's as, storm or no storm, the entire populace of Upsilon appeared to be in the tavern, crammed at tables and cozying up on benches, talking, laughing, drinking, and paying just enough attention to their kids.

Apparently pubs in Stolichnaya were a family affair, serving tea, cocoa, and packets of snacks that would appeal to tiny monsters.

Still, it was odd seeing infants and toddlers bouncing on knees while their older siblings raced between the tables.

"I can't believe the locals build this place, every smogging year." Rory, at Jagati's right, studied the vaulted ceiling which, like the walls, tables, chairs, benches, stools, and bar itself, was made of ice that had been stacked, shaved, or carved from blocks hauled by crawler from the nearby Lake Valhal.

That last detail they'd learned from Keld, the red-bearded bear who'd served their drinks and dropped some knowledge with the booze.

"Not only build it," Kallik, seated on Jagati's other side, raised their glass toward the arched ceiling, "Keld told me that every year the Upsilonians have a contest for the best design, so they construct an entirely different tavern, to different specifications, every year."

"But, why?" Jagati asked.

"Tradition?" Kallik guessed.

"Or just something to do during the cold months," Rory suggested.

"Which probably start in August," Jagati muttered, raising her mug and inhaling the steam from the hot drink Keld swore would thicken her thin, Fordian blood.

Since she'd been too swarming cold to play "my colony's better than your colony," she had taken Keld's suggestion and was glad of it. The drink was not only warming, it was delicious, reminding her a little of Macintosh's famed cider, but with more kick.

With a sigh, she sipped the fragrant liquor and snuggled onto her stool which was, thank the keepers, covered with a thick wool rug, as were all the other stools, chairs, and benches in the place.

It seemed even the rugged citizens of Upsilon resented a cold rump.

Similar rugs hung from the walls, breaking up the unrelieved white of a structure which, combined with the glitter of lanterns throughout, could easily lead to a case of snow blindness.

A loud chorus of, "Skål!" drew her attention to where a group of kids looking for a hangover raised their shot glasses, also made of ice, before downing them all at once. "Don't they worry their lips will freeze to the glass?" she asked no one in particular.

A deep bark of a laugh made her turn to see Keld had returned to their section of the bar.

"Never worry," he said in his Stoli-accented Common. "The alcohol in the drink will keep them safe, as long as they don't linger."

"Or lick the outside," Kallik offered.

"Ack!" Jagati squawked at the image.

"True enough," Keld confirmed with an affable grin. "But there are always some who dare another to try, meaning we keep a kettle on just in case someone needs a glass melted from their tongue."

"Why would anyone do it?" Rory asked. "They'd have to know what would happen."

"Of course," Keld agreed, his great red beard quivering with mirth. "But—who can resist a dare?"

"I can," Jagati decided with a shudder. "What?" she asked as Rory snorted. "I can!"

"Whatever you say," Rory agreed as Keld raised a bottle of Campbell's Best. Both Rory and Kallik held out their tumblers—made of actual glass—for refills.

Once he poured the drinks, Keld used a corkscrew to slash two hashmarks on the ice tablet set before them.

"*Takk*," Kallik said to Keld.

"*Varsa.*" The bartender nodded and took himself down the bar to the next thirsty party.

"Do you speak Stolichnayan?" Rory asked the young doctor.

"Enough to get around," Kallik replied. "'Please, thank you, where does it hurt?' Thanks to Common, being multi-lingual is more an option than a requirement, but I'm also fluent in Inuktiway."

"I've a bit of the Keltican, myself," Rory said, referring to the Campbell Isles' creole.

"I have a friend from university," Kallik said, leaning around Jagati to better see Rory. "She's part of an anthropological linguistic study of the languages of Fortune—Exodus Common and regional alike—tracking the evolution of the spoken word from Earth to present-day Fortune."

"Why?" Jagati asked.

"Because language shapes the way we think, the way we perceive, the way we feel," Kallik said, their eyes alight with interest. "The shape of our thoughts and emotions extend to shaping our societies—how we live, what we value, how we treat one another. So, even though everyone on Fortune learns and uses the Exodus Common specifically developed for a post-Earth society, colonies or states with particularly dense populations from a specific territory of origin often have a second, or even third, more organically mutated creole such as Stolichnayan, Inuktiway, Mejiguese, or Keltican," they added, nodding at Rory. "What Tamara and her team want to determine is how much impact the roots of regional languages have on the people raised in each of those societies—how they view the world, and themselves in it."

"Yeah," Jagati nodded, "make sense, I guess."

"I, for one, would love to know why it is the Midasians are so waste-bent on trickery," Rory muttered. "Nothing is ever what you think with those nobs."

"That could be useful," Jagati said. "But what I want to know is how Avonians got aluminium' from 'aluminum'?"

"While we'd like to know what Fordians have against that wee little i," Rory countered. "What did it ever do to you?"

"I'll be sure to ask Tamara if that comes up in her research," Kallik said with a chuckle before turning their attention to the main tavern. "Eitan's found a new friend," they said with a combination of amusement and appreciation that Jagati would have felt even if she couldn't *feel* it.

"He always does," Rory murmured, and from him Jagati sensed something else—something closer to sorrow.

Or maybe pity?

At which point she realized she was sense-dropping and, with a silent curse, took a moment to reinforce her internal barriers.

Once she felt secure, she followed Kallik's gaze to spy the man himself, seated at one of the ice tables with a party of locals, speaking quietly with a man with weathered skin a few shades darker than Eitan's and whose eyes were milky with cataracts.

As she watched, the blind man laid his gloveless hand on the table, and then Eitan raised that hand to press his lips to the palm.

"Clearly his charm goes beyond his looks," Kallik observed.

"I don't get it," Jagati said, then as both Kallik and Rory shot her wide-eyed looks said, "Not Eitan. I *get* that. I just don't understand how anyone can go without gloves in this joint." She nodded to the bare palm in Eitan's gloved hand. "Even you Mooseheadians are gloved up," she added, glancing at Kallik.

"Well, it's my first ice tavern," Kallik pointed out. "But your captain appears to be comfortable enough without his gloves," they added, nodding at the raised stage near the back of the tavern where John shared a bench with two of the musicians.

Then she saw that John was running his, yes, ungloved fingers, over the strings of a guitar while having a fairly intense conversation with the guitar's owner.

Automatically, she sought out Pyotr and found both he and the drummer—presumably the Soshi he'd come to find—easing through a clutch of drinkers standing near an arched doorway.

"Where are they going?" she asked, gesturing toward Pyotr with her mug.

Kallik followed her gaze. "Maybe there's a snug."

"The ice tavern has a snug?" Jagati's brows hiked up.

Rory glanced her way. "Why wouldn't it?"

"It just seems like an ice tavern's snug wouldn't be very . . ."

"Snuggly?" Kallik offered.

"Exactly." Jagati raised her mug in a toast as Keld returned to their section of the bar.

"So, Keld, do you lot ever get tired of it?" Rory asked, angling to lean his elbows on the slab of ice.

"Of what?" As he spoke, Keld flicked a cloth over his shoulder in the manner of bartenders the world over, leading Jagati to wonder how one wiped down a bar made of frozen water.

"Of seeing all this melt away in the spring." Rory gestured around with his glass. "Do you mourn the loss?"

"But it is not a loss," Keld replied, tapping the bar. "The tavern may melt every spring, but the cycle remains in the people who build it." He gestured to the crowds. "Every year we come together and create a new vision of this place. And every year we gather inside, sharing our achievement. It is a comfort," he added, "knowing we have this *perinne*—this tradition—year after year, generation after generation. It is part of our *elinkaari*, our cycle, you would say." As he spoke, his gaze ran down the line. Seeing a gesture from another customer, he snagged a bottle from beneath the bar and, with a nod to Rory, departed to fill more glasses.

"That's us told," Jagati observed, sipping her drink.

"Maybe," Rory said, then shrugged. "Can't say as I come from a long line of traditions, unless you count the passing down of the family lock picks."

"I think that counts," Kallik decided, just as a fluid run of notes soared above the tables, stilling rumbling waves of conversation throughout.

As one, Jagati, Rory, and Kallik turned to the stage where the harpist, a small woman with close-cropped hair dyed a deep purple, ran her fingers over a lap harp.

"Whoa," Jagati murmured as the liquid notes shivered achingly up her spine.

"You enjoy music, then?"

"Sure, I enjoy music," she replied to Kallik's question. "You don't have to be good at something to enjoy it."

Their eyes twinkled. "And how do you know you are not good at it?"

"Because you need patience to be good," she replied before adding a firm, "Patience is what I am *not* good at."

"Except patience isn't a skill so much as a trait," they said. "And, at least from what I've seen, patience manifests most strongly when a person wants something enough." At which point their gaze shot to the stage, where the strumming of the guitar had joined the harp. "I'd say John has patience to spare, to play as he does."

"John?" Jagati echoed, then turned from the young doctor to the stage, where John was sitting in for the group's guitarist, his head bent over the borrowed instrument as he accompanied the harpist.

And not just plucking out a melody, either.

Even Jagati could see, from the way his fingers moved over the neck, John had skills.

She raised her drink and took a careful sip of the warming liquor.

Not so much because she was thirsty, but because something about seeing him like that, so focused in the moment, and on the instrument in his hands, had her chest turning in a strange way.

How did she not know he played guitar?

Jagati thought back, trying to remember if she'd ever seen an instrument aboard the *Kodiak*, where they'd first served together.

Maybe he'd learned to play later, after the court martial, as a way to ease the pain of being grounded?

Jagati took another sip of her drink, reminding herself it was stupid to feel affronted by this new revelation, this part of John she'd never seen. But she couldn't stop feeling it.

And then her jaw dropped—and the affront fell with it—as John began to sing.

"As I look to the skies above
  I think back to those before
  To the lost and lonely travelers
  whose home was no more . . ."

It was one of the oldest songs on Fortune, penned by one of the descendants of those who originally fled Earth.

"Ten thousand souls sailed a stark and airless sea
  They brought little but their sorrows
  Weighed by sins they dare not repeat."

"They carried a might more than sorrow," Rory observed, dryly. "Else we'd never have a retrieval job."

"And we know at least a few sins that have been repeated," Kallik added. "Otherwise I wouldn't be going to the Stoli border."

"Mmmmph," Jagati grumbled while her hand waved at them to shut it. Her eyes were locked on John, not noticing the glance the other two shared over her head as she leaned forward.

. . .

"They'd never see their harbor
   Their hope lay in a future blind
   They sailed on to a distant promise
   That their children might someday find.

Ten thousand souls
   Sailed a cold and endless sea
   They brought little but their sorrows
   And a hope they'd never meet.

Still they sailed on
   Still they sailed on
   They sailed on to Fortune
   They sailed on home."

As the song came to a close, everyone in the tavern held a collective breath, an instinctive moment of silence to honor those distant ancestors who had taken flight from Earth, knowing they would never live to see Fortune—not even knowing if their descendants would arrive at their promised home. Or, even if they did, that the planet they reached would have been successfully engineered to support human life.

The history books were full of the trials of that mass exodus, including tales of the ships that hadn't survived the journey.

There were songs about those ships, as well.

But the ballad John had sung was more than a history lesson or a reminder of what had been lost on Earth.

It was, in its way, a love song; not to a person, or even a place, but to an idea.

To hope, she supposed.

And as that thought struck, the entire tavern shimmered back to life, first with a series of released breaths, then a few discrete hands flicking at tears, and at last, the thudding rush of hands clapping or striking tables.

It was then, as the thunder of appreciation in the pub rivaled the howl of the wind outside it, that John looked up, his eyes unerringly landing on Jagati's.

Even from the other side of the room, she felt the weight of his gaze, just as she sensed the tug of his longing.

And—even though she wanted to deny it—she felt an answering tug of her own.

Then, as she watched, her heart turning, he handed the guitar to its owner and rose.

As he did, she set her mug aside and slid from her stool.

She heard a low whistle and a soft cheer from Kallik and Rory, respectively.

Any other time, Jagati might have responded with a rude gesture, but here, tonight, all her attention was fixed on the man walking toward her, even as she wove through the tables toward him.

They met halfway, coming to a halt in the middle of the tavern.

Already, the musicians, still minus their drummer, had moved on to another number, a sprightly call and response that encouraged the audience to clap and sing along.

It made for a noisy background, a wash of sound to match the blur of motion around the spot where she stood in front of John, who had yet to take his eyes off hers.

"Why didn't I know you could do that?" she asked, pitching her voice low enough to undercut the raucous music.

"Do what?" he asked, leaning close enough for her to hear the reply. "You'll have to be more specific." And there it was, that little twitch of the cheek that told her a smile lurked in wait.

She hated that lurking smile.

No, she thought, she didn't.

"Smog it," she muttered, and even as her hindbrain shouted, *Bad Idea*, she grabbed John by his open coat and hauled him in, ignoring the hoots and applause from the nearest tables as the kiss shot heat from her crown to her toes, as potent as a drug and as enticing as that first kiss in the cargo bay of the *Errant*.

The only difference being that, this time, she wasn't bleeding out on the deck.

She pulled away, then dove back for more—smog it, the man could kiss!—then pulled away to see John's gaze had gone dark and intense in a way she'd never seen. "Home," she said. "Now."

"Now," he agreed, grasping her hand and angling toward the exit.

The music had picked up its pace, inviting the audience to clap and stomp in time. A few of the crowd had risen to dance as best they could in the limited space.

To Jagati, the noise, the movement, were a faded watercolor, a rush of wind—soft and pale in comparison to the man at her side whose lip was twitching with some unspoken mirth.

"What?" she said, giving him a poke in the shoulder.

The twitch became a grin. "Just thinking. Had I known music would have had this effect, I'd have sung to you years ago."

Jagati snorted, but didn't stop moving for the door. "Won't lie, the singing took me by surprise." She slid him a sideways glance. "I might be asking for a whole lot more entertainment."

"Happy to oblige, as soon as I can get my hands on another instrument," he said, dodging one of the local kids as she dashed between the tables.

"*Whatdidyoujustcallme?*" she responded with a smirk, though even now, she was wondering how many notes they'd be able to strike before the end of the evening.

CHAPTER 6

FROM THE TABLE HE'D JOINED, EITAN WATCHED JOHN and Jagati move toward each other with a purpose that did not require a sensitive to recognize.

"You know him? The fellow who was singing?" one of his table mates asked.

Eitan looked at Yiva, her flaxen braids listing forward as she leaned over her steaming drink. "I do."

"Quite the voice," Magnus observed, reaching unerringly for his glass despite the blindness. "Reminds me of the stories of the sirens of the Amazons."

"I don't believe John would use his voice to lure lost aeronauts to their deaths," Eitan mused, thinking of the centuries' old myths of the seductive mountain spirits, only one of the many tales of the Amazon range disseminated throughout Fortune since First Landing and the loss of the Gamma site.

"Your friend may be no siren," Yiva's partner, Jörn surmised, "but he's lured at least one traveler to his side."

Eitan followed Jörn's gaze to where John and Jagati were now heading toward the exit.

"Hard starbucks say they're about to enjoy a private dance," Yiva offered, raising her mug.

"I don't believe I will take that bet," Eitan said, raising his own glass in a silent toast to his friends. But before he could drink to John and Jagati's fortune, a hooded figure, covered in snow, rushed into the tavern and slammed directly into John before sidestepping and diving into the crowd.

John, being John, shrugged off the contact, and Jagati spared the man a curled lip, but it was obvious her mind was on other business.

The collision may not have slowed either party, but it had caused the newcomer's hood to fall away, revealing a face red from the cold, stubbled with a few days' growth of beard, and eyes that, even from this distance, Eitan knew to be a dark, dark blue.

A dark blue he recognized.

"Conn?" The name fell from his lips even as he rose from his chair.

Jagati, already pushing John toward the door after their brief collision, came to a sudden halt. "Conn?" she asked, turning to stare at the man who'd barreled into them.

"Who?" John asked.

"I don't know," she replied. Glaring at the figure working his way through the crowd, she tried to find the source of her unease but there were just too many bodies in the way, each bubbling with their own stew of emotions.

Her eyes narrowed as she latched on to the cold shock that had first caught her attention, only at the last catching the hint of clove that she associated with Eitan.

She turned to John. "I think Eitan thinks that guy's named

Conn, and something about him is wrong," she said, and added a heartfelt, "Sorry."

She dove back into the tavern while John followed with a muttered, "I can't believe I understood that."

"Something's up," Rory said, straightening from his place at the bar as he watched Jagati spin back and muscle her way through the mass of locals.

"What?" Kallik turned from where they'd been making eyes at a receptive Keld. "Where?"

"Not sure, and there," Rory jerked a chin toward the rear of the pub, where Eitan was on his feet, his expression grim. "Eitan's onto something," he muttered, and hopped off the stool.

"Do you guys do this often?" Kallik asked as they followed.

"Do what?" Rory asked, tugging Kallik closer to avoid being trampled by a pair of dancers ploughing through the tables.

"Look for trouble," they clarified.

"Mostly, 'tis trouble that finds us." Rory ducked under a swinging mug, then ducked again as it swung back in time to the music.

"I get that," Kallik said, wiping spilled mead from their shoulder. "Also, maybe we should try the mead on the way back."

"You're on," Rory said, peering over a furred shoulder to see Eitan diving through an arched door at the rear of the pub. "That way!"

It can't be him. It can't be him. It can't be . . .

The single phrase pounded through Eitan's thoughts as he scythed through the crowd after Conn.

Except it could not be Conn, he again reminded himself as he dove through the open arch into the space behind the stage, where he was immediately struck by the odor of singed flesh.

A quick scan showed the room's single table tipped on one side, both chairs knocked over, and a pile of broken glass glittering against the snow-packed floor.

Beyond the table, he spied a body—the drummer—her eyes glassy with shock, skin pale as the floor on which she lay, a pool of red icing beneath her.

Pyotr knelt at the drummer's side, shooter in hand.

And there, a too-familiar figure was racing through a door that opened to the howling night beyond.

Eitan spared a glance at Pyotr.

"She lives. He can't," the small man said, nodding at the door, all trace of his Stoli accent gone. "Do you understand me Lieutenant Fehr?"

"Not entirely," Eitan said, but as he spoke, he released the spring blade on his left arm and drew his own shooter from beneath his coat.

Then he raced into the howling night, in pursuit of a ghost.

John dodged around a pack of dancers that Jagati tried to plow through, and so managed to enter the room at the back of the tavern mere seconds after Eitan had disappeared.

Smelling the spark of crystal plasma, he came to an abrupt halt and reached for his shooter but was interrupted by someone slamming into him from behind.

"What's going on?" Jagati asked, peeling herself off John. Then she took in the view over John's shoulder of a body down, Pyotr holding his head with one hand and a shooter with the other, and then, on the far side of the room, Eitan racing out into the storm.

She was already drawing her weapon, about to follow, when she was struck from behind.

"Sorry," Rory called as Jagati again rammed into John's back and then, a heartbeat after Rory's apology, another body struck.

"Whoa," Kallik said, then let out a hiss before shoving past the *Errant* crew and dropping to their knees next to the wounded. "Pyotr?"

"I'm fine," Pyotr said, though his voice sounded . . . off.

Kallik appeared to think so as well, offering their companion an odd look before turning back to the woman bleeding out on the snow.

"I could use a med kit," they said calmly, even as they removed their scarf, using it to put pressure on the wound.

"On it," Rory said, and rushed out of the snug.

Since Jagati could see no use for herself in this scenario, she edged around John and made for the exit.

She didn't know if she was pleased or irritated that she heard his steps crunching in the snow behind her.

The cold was a hammer, striking Eitan's lungs with every breath.

The suns had set while he'd been in the tavern, and though the snow had ceased falling, the wind still blew into his narrowed eyes as he scanned the expanse, his shooter steadied over the blade that stood for his left hand.

Movement to his left made him turn, but it was only another elasmothere, this one tethered to a sleigh. The massive creature snorted a cloud while its single horn dipped, and Eitan pushed on.

The faint glow from Upsilon's outmost buildings, along with the hint of moons peering through tattered clouds, gave Eitan a glimpse of a figure moving north, away from the tavern, Upsilon, and the airfield.

He sucked in a breath, the cold spearing his lungs like needles as the would-be killer approached what looked to be a rising shadow . . . and disappeared into it.

That can't be right, he thought, before recalling Magnus and Yiva speaking of one of Upsilon's other winter traditions—the snow Trojeborg.

In the moment, as Yiva had described the project, the scholar in him had found it an interesting and clever way to honor the labyrinths that had originated in many of Earth's cultures.

Now, as he came close enough to see the opening through which his prey had disappeared, the warrior in Eitan experienced a dark appreciation for the fractal nature of a universe which had him, once again, trailing Conn down a pre-ordained path of violence.

***

Kneeling at Kallik's side while the young doctor worked to save a life, Rory had to give credit where due.

Not only was Kallik a skilled field medic, they had no trouble taking command of a potentially explosive situation.

From the moment Rory returned with Keld and the tavern's emergency kit, Kallik had been in control.

And it had been no small feat for the slender physician to keep the burly bartender—or Soshi's bandmates, who'd tumbled in on Keld's heels—from barreling after the *Errant*'s crew in search of the man who'd harmed their friend.

But with the coolest of orders, Kallik had the harpist on the ground with them, keeping pressure on Soshi's wound, the guitarist running to town for the nearest transport, and Keld standing guard, preventing any further incursions into the snug.

Rory, who often served as the ad hoc medic for the *Errant*, decided the best way to be useful would be by tending to the injured Pyotr.

Grabbing a sterile wound pack from the medkit, Rory turned to find the other man, only to discover that Pyotr was nowhere to be seen.

The stillness within the labyrinth surprised Eitan, though it shouldn't have come as a shock that the mounded walls of snow would block the keening wind.

It still sang overhead, but the bite was lessened, as was the sting of the snow it had driven into Eitan's exposed skin.

Hearing the crunch of his own boots in the drifted snow, Eitan stopped, listened and—hearing the crunch of someone else's boots—considered his course.

Unlike the mazes of Epsilon or Guinness, the Trojeborg was a true labyrinth. Not designed to confuse, but to lead the visitor to its center.

Mazes presented many choices, but here there was only the choice between moving forward or moving back.

Eitan chose forward.

They'd just reached the wall of snow into which they'd seen Eitan disappear when Jagati pulled up short and cursed.

"What is it?" John asked, flattening himself against the frigid wall.

"Someone's coming from behind," she hissed.

At that, John turned. "I don't see—"

"Neither do I," she cut him off with a grumble.

"Oh." He paused, cleared his throat. "Can you describe what you're, ah, getting?"

She closed her eyes, sucked in a breath, let it out. "Remember that bag . . . that satchel you carry on every leave?" she asked. "It's like that . . . battered and worn and soft . . . but underneath the leather is the smell you get when you sharpen a knife, the *edgymetallysharpy* thing." Her eyes popped open. "That makes no sense."

"More than you think," John said, and she caught the edges of what felt like frustration, followed by a cool wave that might have been acceptance. "Not to worry," he added, laying a hand on her shoulder—the "go" signal. "If the one following is who I think it is, he's on our side."

As she nodded and moved on, Jagati wasn't entirely sure, but he might have added a soft, *"Mostly."*

Eitan couldn't say how long he'd been moving—a shadow chasing a shadow—when the sound of footsteps he'd been trailing . . . ceased.

With instincts born in battle and honed in the arena, he jumped back, stumbling in a drift of snow as the brief silhouette of a blade pierced the frigid wall, exactly where he had been standing.

The blade's silhouette vanished with a hiss even as Eitan rolled up to one knee to fire his shooter through the packed snow.

The plasma melted a hole in the wall, large enough for Eitan to see his target disappearing to the left.

He fired again, this time melting a gap large enough to dive through, sending a shot to his left as he cleared the passage, forcing his attacker to trip backwards onto the snow-covered ground.

The falling man let out a grunt of pain, reminding Eitan of Pyotr's shooter and the smell of burning flesh from the snug.

Even as he made note of his opponent's injury, the damaged wall rumbled, then collapsed, shooting plumes of white into the air and clumps of hardened snow slithering like waves in Eitan's direction, knocking him from his feet and sweeping his shooter away in the process.

Flipping over, he discovered other man had kept his feet and was even now wading through the piled clumps of snow, raising his sword as he came.

Eitan waited until the sword began to fall before swinging his legs into a scissor kick that forced his opponent to leap back, allowing Eitan to scrabble to his feet in time to meet the next attack.

Sword met spring blade with a dull clang and held, blade to blade, eye to eye.

And so it was that, even in the snow-choked dark, even with all the years between, Eitan could no longer deny the impossible.

"Conn?" he asked, and at the question, the other man hesitated.

Ghost or no, Eitan used that hesitation to his advantage, bringing his right hand in to knock Conn's sword aside while his own blade sliced through the other man's coat sleeve.

Blood flew like ink, spattering the snow as the two men danced away from each other.

It was only then, as he discovered there was enough room to retreat, that Eitan noticed they had reached the center of the labyrinth—an open space anchored by a faintly shimmering pillar of ice—a replica, Yiva had claimed, of the obelisk erected in Alpha, where the first wave of colonists had landed.

Conn let out a soft curse, then flipped the sword to his left hand. "Let me guess," he said, his voice rough as ever, "you know me from somewhere?"

"Know you?" Eitan echoed, then leaped back as Conn's sword sliced at his mid-section. "I suppose you could say that," he replied, whipping around to deliver a kidney punch.

Conn stumbled but quickly pivoted back to guard. "Also guessing we didn't part on good terms?"

"Not the best, no." Eitan feinted to Conn's right, then spun away as Conn riposted with more speed than Eitan recalled.

"And did I do that?" Conn asked, dancing away as he nodded toward the blade which took the place of Eitan's left hand.

"No," Eitan breathed the denial and, without thinking, added, "That happened later . . . after I killed you."

They were deep inside the labyrinth when John heard voices, easily recognizing Eitan's, though he couldn't make out what was being said.

"I smell plasma," Jagati murmured.

"Me too."

And then they rounded a hairpin curve of snow to discover the gaping, melted slump of what had been one of the labyrinth walls.

"Why didn't we think of that?" Jagati asked even as they both heard a distinct, meat-like *thud*.

They looked at each other and, as one, moved toward the collapsed wall.

"You really don't remember?" Eitan asked, pivoting from Conn's last punch to face the next attack.

"I don't remember—" Conn began, but as he met Eitan's gaze, his step hitched, his eyes shifted, and his face—leached of color by the night—seemed to ripple. "I remember the smell of blood, the sound of crowds, cheering? And . . . someone saying I was . . . lucky."

Then he blinked, and his expression changed, smoothed like

sand swept flat by a hand. "But I don't remember you." He sprang forward in a flurry of thrusts and slashes that drove Eitan into the pillar of ice.

His shoulder sang, but still Eitan grabbed Conn's arm, blocking the incoming sword. "You're lying."

Conn blinked and shook his head as if trying to shake off a swarm of bees.

Then, and despite the psionic shields Eitan habitually kept in place, he was slammed by the image of his own face . . . sweating, bleeding, his eyes flickering in the torchlight.

Pain—a hot, wet, tearing—clutched at his gut, as surely it must have clutched Conn's on the long-ago day he'd fallen from Eitan's sword.

"Mothering wasps in the hive!"

"What?" Jagati's curse had John darting around to block her from—he didn't know what. "What's wrong?" he asked while Jagati pressed an arm over her stomach, as if ill or wounded.

"Yeah, Eitan knows this Conn guy," she said, jerking her chin at the two combatants, "and not in a good way."

"Stay here," John ordered, his voice flat as he scrambled over the heap of the collapsed wall.

He should have known she wouldn't listen.

Gritting his teeth, Eitan slammed his head into Conn's nose, then reared back to kick him in the chest, sending the other man flying backwards before punching his own thigh, hard, in an attempt to dispel Conn's fevered memories of the past.

But here, in the deadly cold of the present, Conn barely took a breath to recover before charging forward, sword whistling overhead.

Eitan dropped where he stood, slashing at Conn's legs at the same time Conn's sword whistled overhead, slicing into the pillar. A rain of ice pattered down the back of Eitan's coat while Conn danced back, leaving a trail of dark spots from the fresh cut in his thigh.

In the same moment, a flurry of motion from the left told Eitan his crewmates had arrived.

"Don't," he shouted, not even looking at them.

Jagati might have been able to ignore John's glare as she joined him—and by now, he really should have known she wouldn't listen—but she couldn't so easily shrug off Eitan's harsh order as he engaged with the enemy.

Some might say Eitan's opponent had the advantage, seeing as he had two hands and the build and balance of a natural brawler.

But Jagati knew better.

Just as she knew that, as close to equal as these two men appeared, Eitan was holding back.

Not much—not so much that most would even notice—hells, she wasn't even sure Eitan noticed.

But she did.

Unaware of his crewmate's assessment of the battle, Eitan parried Conn's latest thrust with a moulinet, and followed it up with a combined slash and punch to the plasma burn in Conn's side.

Conn fell back and spared a glance for Eitan's friends who remained still, stark as pencil sketches against the white walls.

Conn, squaring off, indicated the watching pair.

"Backup?" he asked.

"Eitan doesn't need—" John began

"Like he needs backup," Jagati scoffed at the same time.

John shook his head, and imagined Jagati's eyes rolling, as Conn's face split into a grin and the fog of Eitan's pained breath added a dreamlike quality to the battle.

A battle that—or so John thought—held a kind of familiarity, of the sort one saw in dancers who'd partnered a long time.

He could almost see the echo of previous engagements as the two combatants clashed, Eitan parrying blade to blade while twisting the other man's arm and sending him toward the pillar.

Conn using that momentum to pivot into a punto reverso.

Eitan's answer was to close distance, so for a moment, John had only the impression of two dark figures merging against the white background before one broke away, sending a splatter of dark drops onto the snow.

"Just like old times," Eitan said, shaking off the graze to his ribs as Conn, with a fresh wound to the hip, angled to keep Eitan in view.

"So you say," Conn hissed, but this time the casual dismissal was forced.

Jagati shook her head as Conn's emotions slammed into her like an avalanche—a *roughburlappyfriendly* sensation twined with a shimmer of respect, slicked over an ephemeral sweetness—a foreboding of decay.

When her vision finally cleared, Eitan and Conn's positions had reversed. Conn's sword extended in a thrust that Eitan blocked—and here Jagati privately swore she would buy Rory *all the drinks* for building that spring dagger for their friend—before Eitan reared back into a leaping kick to Conn's sternum.

The blow sent Conn back into the pillar, and Eitan followed, grabbing Conn's arm and slamming it into the obelisk, again and again until the blade dropped to the snow, leaving the two men locked together, breath fogging the air between them.

———

"Well?" Conn demanded, his eyes a dark, unreadable pool as they met Eitan's. "What are you waiting for?"

In response, Eitan kicked the sword away. "There is no one forcing me, this time," he said, straightening, but then had to brace himself as Conn grabbed Eitan's left arm, pulling the spring blade toward himself.

"No," Eitan said, twisting the point to the side. "Not again."

"Please," Conn said, his normally rusty voice harsh with desperation. "Please—end this."

Eitan winced as the plea sliced the air between them, keener than any blade. "I can't."

"I can," a voice, almost familiar, broke through the tableaux.

Eitan heard John's "No," and Jagati's curse as Conn shoved him to the side.

Stumbling, Eitan straightened in time to see the plasma bolt strike Conn in the chest, throwing him into the pillar once more, this time to slump, a puppet without his strings, to the snow.

CHAPTER 7

EITAN SPUN FROM CONN'S BODY, BLOOD IN HIS EYES, to see the man who was even now wrestling through the slumped wall of snow. "Pyotr?" he breathed the name. "You didn't have to kill him."

"Yes, I did," Pyotr replied, his breathing labored. "Especially once it became clear you wouldn't."

"What?" Jagati turned from the fallen Conn to glare at Pyotr. "Wait, where's the accent?"

Rather than respond, Pyotr shot a look at John, who sighed. "Pyotr isn't Stolichnayan," he explained, holstering his shooter. "Or Pyotr, for that matter."

"What?" Jagati said again, and though she peppered John with questions, Eitan heard none of them.

All he knew in the moment was the cold slithering through the slice in his coat, up his sleeve, and down the back of his neck.

He thought his face might actually have frozen.

"You've been wounded," Jagati said, and Eitan realized she was standing at his side. "We need to get you inside."

"Not yet," that almost familiar voice interrupted, and both Eitan and Jagati turned to see Pyotr stooping to pick up Eitan's fallen shooter. As they all watched, he fired three shots, melting streaks in the white walls and scoring the churned snow on the ground before tossing it at John, who caught it automatically. "We need to search the body," he ordered.

"Search?" Jagati's question was as hot as the plasma Pyotr had fired. "For what?"

"For whatever he took from Soshi," Pyotr explained as John also knelt at Conn's side, where both men began rifling through the dead man's pockets.

"Law's coming," Jagati warned as the sounds of shouts began to filter over the top of the surrounding walls.

"I haven't found anything," Pyotr said.

"Nothing here either," John agreed.

"Get me another minute," Pyotr said to John, who rose and sloughed through the snow to meet the oncoming figures, two of them armed, who'd appeared in the fallen wall.

"Keld," John greeted as the tavern's bartender, lamp held high, stepped over the humps of snow and nodded at the two women in uniform. "Officers. Thank you for arriving so soon, though as you can see, the threat has been . . . dealt with."

As he spoke, John indicated the signs of battle while blocking Pyotr's activities from the newcomers.

Eitan felt a spike of shock and turned to Jagati, who was gaping at John's performance. He nudged her with his elbow, and she shut her mouth hard enough he heard her teeth clack.

Then they both listened to John describing a desperate battle that included Conn being in possession of Eitan's shooter— which John handed over to the two police officers for inspection.

It all sounded like something out of a quarterstar dreadful, but somehow John made it all seem plausible. "Pyotr had no choice," John concluded. "If he hadn't fired, that man may well have killed Eitan."

Eitan was moving almost before John finished the sentence.

This time, Jagati nudged him while the word *"trust"* rang in his brain so clearly, she might as well have said it aloud.

He didn't want to trust, but by now Pyotr was standing, looking at John and shaking his head.

Eitan and Jagati both saw John acknowledge the gesture before turning to the police. "Perhaps we can answer any further questions somewhere else?" he suggested. "As you can see, both Eitan and Pyotr could use medical assistance."

"Dr. Natsiq-Corvais is still at the tavern," Keld said. "They were—amazing—in the way they helped Soshi."

"Amazing," Jagati echoed, but the look that she shot John made it clear, at least to Eitan, she wasn't referring to Kallik's skills.

John met her gaze, then Eitan's before offering a resigned, "I could use a drink."

<hr>

In the end, John skipped the drink.

Best all around, he decided, what with the local constables wanting answers.

Answers neither Jagati nor Eitan liked but, given that only Pascal had the vaguest idea why the stranger had attacked Soshi, playing ignorant wasn't so very far from the truth.

We're berthed at the air dock, waiting out the storm.

No, I've never seen the man before.

Yes, Pyotr acted in haste, but he had no choice.

Most of which was true enough.

Pascal stuck with the theme of shock and horror, and while Kallik cleaned and bandaged his head, declared their attacker must have been snow mad or some such, for who would want to harm Soshi?

And Eitan, who seemed to have actually known the dead man,

explained he thought he'd recognized him as a friend from the war but had been mistaken.

Their statements didn't shed much light on the situation, but the officers were satisfied everyone from the *Errant* had done their best in a bad situation. And, as Kallik's quick action had saved Soshi's life, they were all released with the gratitude of the local police force and a bottle of vodka from Keld.

By the time they left the tavern, the storm had fully abated, and the shredded clouds parted enough for the moons, suspended in a glittering field of stars, to light their way back to the airfield.

The cold was sharp as glass, the only sounds their boots crunching in the snow.

John sighed, his breath turning to fog, and wondered what sort of intelligence Soshi had meant to pass to Pascal, and where said intelligence might have ended up, as there had been nothing on the body but a knife, a garrote, and a flask.

No shooter, no money, no rations. No pocket litter at all.

All of which meant the man couldn't have traveled far on foot.

Which meant he'd been staying in Upsilon, or had arrived on another airship, as the trains didn't run this far north.

John further wondered which of the Colonies' many enemies Conn worked for. Then he glanced at Eitan, striding forcefully through the airfield gates, and decided to leave those wonderings to Pascal.

He was more than relieved when they reached the *Errant*, still softly bobbing at anchor and, with Rory's aid, hauled open the cargo bay door.

They'd barely stepped into the 'ship when Kallik insisted on taking Eitan to the medbay.

"It is only a graze," Eitan told them, repeating the assertion he'd made in the tavern.

"Odd," Kallik observed, "I don't see anyone else here with a medical degree."

"I'd listen to them," Jagati added, earning a glower from Eitan and a wink from the doctor.

"Meanwhile I'd best run up to the envelope and check the anterrium cells for storm damage," Rory said, handing Keld's vodka to Kallik.

"Good idea," John agreed. "Maybe we'll be lucky enough to raise anchor tomorrow."

At that, Pascal glanced up at John—clearly the operative wasn't happy with the idea of leaving Upsilon without Soshi's intel.

Given John wasn't happy with the way the evening had turned out, that seemed only fair.

Several minutes later Jagati watched from the medbay door while Kallik dug out the *Errant*'s suture kit and Eitan doffed his coat, scarf, sweater, tunic, and unbuckled his spring blade.

Staring at the blade, she hoped it wasn't obvious how annoyed she was at John and Pyotr—or whatever his name really was—for running off together.

How dumb do they think we are?

John knows better.

Jagati almost jumped at that thought, which sounded suspiciously like Eitan's voice but inside her head.

Taking a steadying breath, she looked at Eitan, sitting on a cot while Kallik cleaned his wound, and saw an echo of her own surprise.

Because while both were sensitives, never before had her empathy and his telepathy merged the way it had over the past couple of hours.

"Ugh," she groused aloud, before she thought better.

Kallik shot her a puzzled look while Eitan sighed.

"Would you prefer to wait in the galley?" Kallik asked, likely assuming Jagati found the sight of someone being sutured gross. She had to give them full marks for not sounding even a little judgmental.

"Actually, I could use a cup of tea," Eitan said.

"Ah, yeah . . . of course." Jagati straightened. "I'll get that set up and meet you in the galley when you're done." *Yeah, I am so smooth,* she thought, rolling her eyes at herself as she left.

Still, the task gave her something to do, and by being the one making the tea, she got to choose the blend.

Rory was fond of some yellow flowery tea at night, but it tasted like chewing on sadness to her, so she made her normal Fujian black, brewed strong enough to wake a hibernating bear.

Once it had steeped sufficiently, she poured herself a cup, took a bracing sip, and let the questions roiling through her mind bubble to the surface.

Questions like, who was Pyotr, really?

What kind of history did Pyotr and John share?

Since both of those questions required either John or Pyotr to answer, she deliberately left them in a corner to think about what they'd done and moved on to wondering if she had really heard Eitan's voice in the medbay.

Had she truly touched minds with Conn while in the labyrinth? That moment of connection—the hot, ripping agony of Eitan's sword—visceral didn't even begin to, ha, cut it.

And later, when she'd stopped Eitan from charging into John's explanation to the cops—she'd said nothing, only thought the word, *trust*—and Eitan had stopped.

"Or Eitan just knows John well enough to actually trust him," she muttered, warming up her tea. Then, upon hearing footsteps on the starboard deck, she reached for a second mug.

"You'll need rest," she heard Kallik say, their own voice weary.

"And I will, but—"

"But adrenaline, and anger, and pride," Kallik cut in, though

Jagati felt there was a smile in their voice. "I've worked with a few veterans. Be well, Eitan."

There was a pause, long enough that Jagati started to put the second mug back in the cupboard, then Eitan murmured something too low to hear, his words followed by a single set of footsteps on the ladder and another set of footsteps approaching the galley.

By the time Eitan entered, she was holding out a steaming mug. "Not sure how serious you were about the tea, but here it is."

"It could not possibly hurt," he said, dropping his coat, sweater, scarf, and blade on the table before taking the offered beverage. "To walking off the field of battle," he raised the mug with the infantry toast.

"To jumping another day," she returned, jumper to the last.

After another sip, she snuggled the mug to her chest for warmth. "So? Your take on Pyotr . . . and John?"

Eitan glanced at the galley doors, then sighed and leaned back against the counter at Jagati's side. "I would say Pyotr not being Pyotr indicates he works for an agency outside Medics Beyond Borders. And," he added, "that he and John have a history."

She grunted in agreement and frustration. "I got that the first time we met the doctors, when John almost passed a draco the second whatever his name really is showed up." And covered it just as quickly, she thought with an uncomfortable lurch. "Don't like it."

"Which part?" Eitan asked. "That John has secrets or that you now know it?"

"Both," she snapped, then smirked at her own ridiculousness. "How dare he keep something from me . . . and so well that I had not one smogging clue." Her tone was light, but it didn't quite counter the pit in her stomach.

At her side, Eitan contemplated his mug before at last admitting. "I too, am angry."

As a complex scent of burning spices infiltrated his statement, she was inclined to believe him.

"But," he continued, angling his head only just enough to meet her eyes, "I also know that I have secrets I would as soon no one else ever learned." He didn't quite pause, but in that half-a-heartbeat she recalled heat and blood and Eitan's face twisted in something she thought to be grief as Conn fell from his sword before he added, "'Leave your past on the ground,' isn't that what they say in the Air Corps?"

"Fair enough," she muttered, then took another sip of tea before shaking her head. "No," she decided, thunking her mug on the counter. "This isn't the same. This Pyotr thing tangled up our entire crew . . . not to mention the doctors."

"And Conn," Eitan murmured. "Somehow."

"And Conn," she agreed, rapping the counter with her knuckles. "I say we go find Pyotr and, and—"

And what? she thought. "—find out why Conn had to die twice."

At which point Eitan almost dropped his mug—would have, if Jagati hadn't snapped her hand out to steady his.

"I didn't think that," she said, releasing his hand once she saw he'd steadied.

"No," he agreed, his dark eyes flat as he added, "But I did."

"Okay, that's"—her hands flailed—"whatever, let's go find Pascal and John and get some damn answers."

Eitan hissed, then shrugged. "Why not?" he asked before taking a hefty swallow of his tea and thumping the mug next to hers. "It's obvious we'll not be sleeping for some time anyway." He grabbed his gear from the table as they headed for the port arch before asking. "Do you *have* to brew the tea half to death?"

"If your spoon can't stand up in it, why bother drinking it?"

CHAPTER 8

PASCAL LED JOHN TO HIS ASSIGNED QUARTERS, WHERE the doorknob felt like ice to fingers already stiff from the cold. Rubbing his hands together, Pascal automatically skimmed the tells he'd set in place before heading out to the tavern.

The slip of paper in the drawer, the strand of hair on his pillow, the thread at the door of the closet, all in place. Pascal glanced into the small head, where the fragrant cedar soap lay *just so* in front of his shaving kit, which in turn was propped *just so* on the edge of the sink.

"All clear?" John asked, reminding Pascal that the *Errant*'s captain had some familiarity with tradecraft.

"All clear," he replied, heading for the desk to open one of the drawers, from which he drew a bottle, along with a stacked set of copper cups.

"Still traveling prepared," John observed, then cocked an eyebrow. "Favreau's Familiar?" His lip turned up in the hint of a smile. "Not very Stolichnayan."

"An old friend introduced Pyotr to Favreau," Pascal said. "Which is true enough," he added, shooting John a glance as he opened the bottle.

"That was quite an evening," John reminisced.

"It was quite a mission," Pascal amended, handing John a cup before filling one for himself. "To Siqiniq."

"To Siqiniq," John echoed the name of a comrade, long deceased, and then both men drank.

Pascal let the woodsy malt glide over his tongue. He closed his eyes, the better to savor the slow spread of heat from the liquor as he swallowed.

A brief respite, but a much needed one, and over as soon as he heard the *clink* of John's cup on the desk.

With a sigh, Pascal opened his eyes to see John taking a seat on the neatly made bed. "What do you want to know?"

"Everything," John said, but with that hint of a smile. "And nothing." He leaned forward to rest his arms on his legs. "I'd forgotten, or told myself I'd forgotten, how Special Operations works."

"You were good at it," Pascal recalled. "Your eye for detail, your curiosity . . . your painfully honest face." He paused, set his cup down. "What did it, in the end?" he asked, meeting that honest face. "What made you transfer? Sorry." He waved his own question aside. "You don't have to say."

"I think maybe I do," John said, but even so, it was a moment before he continued. "I left because . . . because I was so good at it. It became too easy to slide into whoever, whatever, was necessary to do the needful." And as Pascal watched, something, some shadow, passed over John's face as he added, "And that—it being so easy—struck a little too close to home."

At which point Pascal remembered again that night, long ago, with John and Siqiniq—lost during that same mission—and a bottle of Favreau's Familiar, and the truths all three had spilled as the bottle emptied. "Your father," he murmured, understanding.

"I was still young enough to worry," John agreed.

"Corps healers are the best. They would have sensed—"

"The healers never lived with him." John shook his head.

"Even without that baggage, I found I didn't like who I was in Spec Ops, and there were other ways to serve." Then he caught himself and met Pascal's gaze. "I'm sorry."

"Don't be." Pascal, who never would have been accepted into the Infantry and would have to seek accommodations for the Air Corps, shrugged. "I do like who I am in Spec Ops."

"And you are good at it."

"Most of the time," Pascal said, absently rubbing at his forehead, only to wince when he struck the dressing at his temple.

"How bad is it?"

He looked at John. "You don't just mean my head, do you?"

"Your head is made of granite, so no. I mean this—whatever—Soshi was delivering? And how did Conn know to look for her in the first place?"

"That's the thousand starbuck question." Pascal leaned back against the desk. "Soshi told me the intel was delivered by a runner from Kopernik, who received it from a Isroan asset. Given the way this Conn came in—you wouldn't believe it," he said as the scene replayed in his memory. "His sword was out when he walked into the snug—he stabbed Soshi, grabbed her tipper, and threw the drum at me before I could even draw my shooter."

"But he knew to attack Soshi," John pointed out.

"Yes, which makes me fear the Kopernik runner's body is also out there, somewhere." Pascal turned to look out the port.

"I wonder—"

A soft knock and a hissed, "We know you're in there!" was followed by the door swinging open.

Eitan and Jagati strode into the room like twinned thunderclouds.

"What took you so long?" John asked, clearly unsurprised by his crew's invasion.

"Eight stitches," Eitan said.

"And tea," Jagati added, starting to close the door, but a soft

"Oi!" stopped her, and then Rory came sidling into the room, which was suddenly quite crowded.

Smog it, but this crew is tall, Pascal thought.

"I thought you were checking the anterrium cells for damage?" Jagati asked the engineer as Eitan crossed to the far side of the bed.

"I was," Rory said, easing past her to stake a claim in front of the closet. "No troubles up top, but," he added with a quick glance at Pascal, "I bet there are some here."

"There will be if we don't get some explanations." Jagati closed the door and planted herself in front of it, as if daring anyone to escape.

Pascal looked from the small invasion to John. "I suppose some introductions are in order."

"Ya think?" Jagati growled.

John simply shook his head, as if accustomed to frayed tempers and surly first mates. "Everyone, this is Major Pascal Ouellet, Colonial Special Operations," he said, waving at Pascal. "Pascal—well, you already know everyone."

"I'd say it's a pleasure," Pascal offered, "but I get the feeling you'd disagree."

"Maybe we would be pleased, if we'd been kept in the loop from the start," Jagati snapped.

"Maybe you could say that a little louder," Pascal countered, keeping his voice low. "I'm not sure your voice reached Kallik's room." Which was across the corridor and two doors aft from Pascal's.

"Listen," she said, stepping forward, only to halt when John raised a hand.

This time she hissed, but returned to her self-appointed post at the door.

"I believe Jagati's point," Rory stated, "is that if you'd told us you had a mission, we could have been on guard."

"Spies tend, on the whole, not to tell people that they're engaged in the act of spying," Pascal pointed out.

"But John knew," Eitan said. He looked at John. "The way you behaved in the labyrinth, and after. You knew who Pascal was and what he was doing."

"John knows me from our days working together in Spec Ops," Pascal said before John could reply.

"What?" Jagati asked.

"Whoa." Rory straightened.

Eitan said nothing.

Pascal looked at John. "You didn't tell them?"

"Leave your past on the ground," John muttered. "It's not just a motto."

"Of course not." Pascal shook his head. "I'm sorry," he said to everyone before focusing on Eitan. "I'm especially sorry for your friend. And more, I'm sorry I have to ask you—who was he? This isn't me being petty," he said as Jagati let out a soft curse. "I can be," he added, "but not this time. Please," he continued, focusing on Eitan's dark gaze, "Who was he?"

Eitan took a breath, released it, then he too folded himself onto the bed. The mattress creaked under his weight, and he set his blade and his coat carefully aside before angling towards Pascal. "Conn was another POW in Adia," he said at last. "We became friends . . . as much as one can, in the Domino arena. He'd been cavalry, and I was infantry, so we . . . had a rivalry going, the way people do. Our cells were close, and we had practice together, meals together—were occasionally partnered in the arena."

Here he paused, but Pascal knew there would be more, and he was right.

"I knew he was the eldest child of two," Eitan continued, "that his parents were a weaver and a river woman, respectively, and that Conn was looking forward to going home and setting up a tavern." As he spoke, Eitan's eyes seemed to focus on something, or someone, else. "He wanted to have a place of his own, but more, he wanted to be part of something that would make people happy. He was always keen for a joke, and was proud of his sister, who was studying medicine in Epsilon.

"And then, one day, both our names were drawn for a death match—a practice the Adians adopted shortly before the war's end—which means the last time I saw Conn was when he was bleeding out on the arena floor, and I had been declared the victor."

There was a moment of silence following that, but as much as Pascal might have to say about the Adians and their toxic traditions, there simply wasn't time. "If you're correct," he said, "and the man in the labyrinth was Conn—"

"It was," Eitan and Jagati said at the same time.

"Right," Pascal said after a beat. "If that's the case, then he was also, at one time, a Colonial soldier." He paused, took a breath, then asked, "What would have made him turn?"

At the question, he heard John, Jagati, and Rory all sucking in a breath, but Eitan simply shook his head. "I don't know. The Conn I knew . . . he wasn't what I would call overly patriotic, but he loved his home, his people. But this—the man in the labyrinth —he was not the same. And, again, the last time I saw him, I thought—I was sure—he'd died."

"Maybe he did," John murmured. "In all the ways that matter."

"Then who was that out there?" Jagati asked.

"What remains," Pascal said, then shook his head. "There are ways to break a mind, and keepers know it happens, more often than Command would like to admit."

"That's not disturbing at all," Rory observed.

"Tell me," Pascal agreed. "Still, however Conn was lost, he successfully intercepted the information Soshi meant to deliver." He sighed, just stopping himself from rubbing at the dressing on his head. "I don't know if we can leave without some idea what happened to that tipper."

"Tipper?" Jagati echoed, visibly confused. "Like a kid who knocks over sleeping aurochs?"

There was a moment of silence before Pascal said, "No."

"It's actually more of a—" John began.

"'Tis the *cipín* he means," Rory said, then turned to face Pascal as he reached into his pocket and withdrew a piece of slender wood carved with a thick grip in the center and bulbs at either end.

"Keepers in the apiary," Pascal breathed. "How—where did you find it?" he asked.

"In the snug, half under the table." Rory eyed the traditional striker used by bodhran players the world over. "At the time, I was surprised it didn't break, given the crack in the middle." As he spoke, he held up the *cipín* for everyone to see that there was, indeed a thin line bisecting the central grip. "Then I realized it wasn't a crack at all, but a seam." He looked at Pascal. "Clever place to hide something, if the something's small enough."

"This would have been," Pascal muttered, then glared at Rory. "Did you open it?"

"Not yet."

"I wouldn't," John said.

"I would," Jagati countered.

"By all means, if you want to be sworn in as an asset," Pascal told her.

"You're already using us," Jagati snapped, then lowered her voice to add, "so why not?"

"Because the pay is lousy, and you strike me as someone with authority issues," Pascal told her.

"Can confirm," John murmured.

"Wouldn't any message be in code?" Eitan asked.

"Likely," John said.

"Definitely," Pascal admitted. "But, as you've all proven more than able to adapt, improvise, and run with a hunch," here he again eyed Jagati, "I wouldn't advise it."

"Then what would you advise?" Jagati's voice was cloaked in patience, belied by the arms she crossed over her chest.

"To begin?" Pascal turned from Jagati to Rory. "I recommend you hand over the tipper."

Rory turned to John, so Pascal also looked at John, waiting.

John nodded, and Pascal turned back to Rory.

Rory handed the tipper across the bed, and into Pascal's waiting hand.

"Wait," Jagati said.

"First landers preserve us." Pascal rolled his eyes. "Why?"

"Because I can feel your doubts," she explained through gritted teeth. "If you don't trust us, we can't trust you. What are you worried about?"

"Everything," Pascal said. "All the time. Because that's my job. And right now, I'm worried about whatever is in this tipper, which has led to at least one death, that we know of."

And with that, and a deft twist, he unscrewed the top half of the stick, revealing a narrow, tightly rolled slip of paper which he read quickly, then read again.

He muttered a curse, rolled it up, slid it back into the tipper, and closed it up.

Finally, he looked at Eitan. "It is in code," he said, then turned to John. "This information needs to be delivered to General Satsuke, in person."

"We can drop you off on the way back from Kopernik—" John began.

"No," Pascal said. "I can't return with you. I have to go to Kopernik." He glanced at the tipper, brow furrowed. "My cover is intact, so far, and if the information in this message is correct, I need to see what is happening in Isroa."

"Not to play silly buggers," Rory said, "but you wouldn't happen to know where yon general is at this particular point in time? So we're not flying hither and yon after her?"

"Last we spoke, she was to fly to Epsilon," Pascal said. "But I can confirm that before you lift off from Kopernik."

"Assuming we agree to make delivery," John said.

At which point Pascal, and everyone else in the room, turned to stare.

"You mean you'd say no?" Pascal asked.

"Why would I say yes?" John asked back.

"It's your—"

"If you're going to say it's my duty, let me remind you that I was court martialed and drummed out of the Corps for doing my duty. At present, my duty is to my crew and my 'ship, and my crew has already bled for you, so your arguments in favor are . . ." John held out his hand, palm down, and waggled it.

Pascal's eyes narrowed. "John, are you attempting to blackmail the Corps?"

"I suppose I am," John said, and appeared altogether too proud of himself.

Then again, Pascal was feeling little tingles of pride himself, which was odd, until he saw Jagati's face, heard Eitan's throat clearing, and the tingles shut off like a light switch.

Sensitives, he thought, and looked over to John, still seated on the bed. Not, Pascal knew, because he was tired, but because by sitting it spared Pascal from always having to look up to meet his eyes.

It was, all in all, a very John thing to do.

"Very well," he conceded, with his own faint smile. "And what would it cost to persuade you to make a delivery to Epsilon?"

John named his price, which was followed by Rory letting out the quietest whoop of joy Pascal had ever heard.

Jagati's face was a blank as she stared at John, while Eitan's expression became, if possible, even more closed.

Pascal, for his part, gave a short nod. "I can't promise, you understand, but I will do everything I can to see the Corps meets your asking price."

"Good enough." John said, holding out a hand for the tipper.

CHAPTER 9

Three days later, John hauled a crate down the gangplank to where a crawler painted in the Medics Without Borders blue and green waited.

The skies were clear, the suns bright, and the Kopernik air frigid—February in Stolichnaya—but it lacked the angry bite of Upsilon's storm.

As he arrived at the crawler where Jagati and Eitan were assisting with load in, John figured they would all be recovering from that bite for some time to come.

Bypassing the crawler's ramp, he placed his crate on the bed for Jagati to lift and hand off to Kallik who, with Eitan, secured it among the rest of the supplies they'd been loading.

Pascal, once again in his guise as Pyotr, sat on the edge of the bed, ticking off the supplies as they arrived.

"Was that the last?" Alain asked, coming from the crawler's cockpit, Lakshmay at his side.

"Not quite," Pascal said, then looked up to where Rory was muscling a dolly stacked with boxes of tinned goods across the field.

"But that is."

"Oh, good," Kallik said as they peered out over Pascal's head. "I don't know how we could have survived without a season's worth of vat-grown salmon."

"They were donations from the Nike plant," Alain said, eyeing his offspring.

"And they chose to donate the one protein they can't convince anyone to buy," Kallik pointed out.

"Buck up, doc," Jagati said, giving Kallik a thump on the shoulder. "Pretty sure I saw a sizable crate of seasonings stowed in the back."

"Not enough spice on Fortune," Kallik muttered.

Jagati grinned, shook her head. "Be careful out there," she said to the young doctor. "And," she added, hopping down to the ground to shake Lakshmay's hand, "holler if you need us."

"Who are you, and what have you done with my first mate?" John asked, then wished he'd said nothing as her eyes flicked to him and away again, reminding him that, while the doctors might have been admitted into her carefully curated circle, he himself had been relegated to the perimeter.

The sound of a throat clearing drew John's attention back to the crawler where Pascal, still seated, was digging into a satchel. "Before we leave, I wanted to be sure you had this," he said, the Stolichnayan accent in full force as he pulled a bottle out of the bag.

Kallik leaned over the other man's shoulder. "Favreau's Familiar?"

"Not vodka?" Alain asked, leaning against the crawler.

"Captain Pitte is from Moosehead," Pascal explained. He held out the bottle. "An old friend introduced me to Favreau's," he continued, "and I thought it would be to your liking."

"Your friend has good taste," John said, looking up to meet Pascal's gaze, which, being Pascal, was thoroughly unenlightening. John took the bottle. "Thank you."

"No," Pascal said quietly. "Thank you."

Once hands had been gripped over the deal, the rest of the crew filed out of Pascal's quarters, leaving John alone with his old colleague.

"So," Pascal said.

"So," John echoed.

They looked at one another. "For what it's worth, I'm sorry," Pascal said.

"For which part?"

Pascal shrugged. "All of it. But mostly, for ruining your chances with Jagati."

John frowned, replaying their evening in the tavern. "You were already in the snug," he pointed out. "How did you know we were—that we meant . . ."

"Please," Pascal waved at John, "I don't need to be a sensitive to read frustrated lust. Though," he glanced at the door, then back, "I suspect it's more than lust, isn't it?"

"Much more," John said, then added, "It always has been, with her."

"I truly am sorry," Pascal said and, John knew, meant it. "But—well, that's how it goes with this job, and the job is bigger than me." There was a pause before he continued, "This is where you're supposed to say that everything is bigger than me."

John managed a smile. "That joke was worn to a thread a decade ago."

"Siqiniq didn't think so."

"Siqiniq was, on occasion, an ass."

"Truer words," Pascal agreed, then picked up the bottle of Favreau's. "Another drink?"

"May as well."

Four days out of Kopernik, Rory followed the rest of the *Errant* crew through Epsilon Base. He took a deep breath of the chill morning air and tried to settle his nerves.

The last time he'd traversed the airfield in Epsilon, he, Jinna, and Liam had still been serving on the *York*.

It wasn't long after that day that Jinna had become pregnant with Liam's child, Rory had resigned from the Air Corps, and Liam had taken 'ship for the Amazon mountain range, where the *York* had gone down with all hands.

As they entered a building in the center of the base, he wondered if the ache of Liam's passing would ever ease.

"Here we are." Their guide, an ensign young enough to have missed most of the fighting, paused at the door to an office. "I'll be waiting outside to escort you back to the airfield gate," she added.

"Like we don't know where it is," Jagati muttered.

"Regulations," John muttered back.

"As you say, sir," the ensign agreed, even as the door to Satsuke's office popped open to reveal a handsome man of medium height with long black hair tied back in a tail.

"Ah, Ensign Ndlaze, thank you."

"My pleasure, Colonel," Ndlaze replied before stepping back and sliding into parade rest.

"Come in, please," the man said, pulling the door further open for the crew.

Rory, last in line, got a glimpse of what he supposed was a waiting room—a small desk, some chairs along the wall, a low table, maps on the walls—before their host spoke again. "I am Colonel Saeng Tenjin," he introduced himself, before turning to John. "Captain Pitte. It's an honor. Major Ouellet speaks highly of you."

John offered a ghost of a smile as Tenjin moved on to Jagati. "My wife served as a jump master on the *Phalanx*, before transferring to S.O. She'll be sorry she missed this meeting." As Jagati's brow rose, he smiled. "She enjoys reminiscing with others who willingly leap out of airships with nothing but a slender line preventing them from becoming a blot on the landscape."

Jagati grinned. "It's not that bad."

"Yes, it is," John said, and he and the colonel shared an understanding glance.

Tenjin turned his attention to Eitan. "Lieutenant Fehr. Welcome back to the land of the living."

Eitan nodded, seemed inclined to say nothing else, and Tenjin appeared to be fine with that as he angled toward Rory. "Msr McCabe. You may not know it, but your assessment of the *Odysseus* has become a case study for new recruits in Spec Ops."

"The—my—*oh*," Rory said, which was all he could manage, as he recalled the Midasian airship, discovered on the fields of southern Stolichnaya in the last years of the war.

Rory's captain at the time had wanted to repair the 'ship and fly it back to Epsilon. Rory, though, had prior experience with Midasians and had warned against it. His warnings, Rory knew, would have fallen on deaf ears had Lieutenant Liam Del not supported Rory's assessment.

In the end, Rory, Liam, and Airborne Specialist Jinna Pride had been dispatched to search the 'ship prior to any action, and had discovered that the *Odysseus* to have been mined with casks that, had they blown, would have infected everyone aboard with Midasian fever, likely leading to a serious outbreak in the Corps, if not the Colonies themselves.

It had been quite a day, and had ended in Rory, Liam, and Jinna becoming friends—and more than friends—though at the time, Rory hadn't realized how much more.

"It was good work, on all your parts," the colonel said, then added a quiet, "My sorrow for your loss."

"Thank you," Rory said, curbing the swell of confused feelings that always arose around thoughts of Liam, and counted himself lucky when the connecting door opened and a wee woman with silver-streaked hair leaned out to say, "Oh. Good. You're all here."

Two days after dropping the doctors in Kopernik, Rory knocked on John's cabin door.

"Come in!"

"Eitan said you wanted to see me?" he asked, peeking through the door.

"I did." As he spoke, John pushed away from his desk, grabbed a slip of telgram tape, and held it out. "You received a message from Jinna."

"Is she well? Is it the baby?" Rory shoved the spanner he'd been holding into his back pocket. Taking the tape, he gave John a look. "Don't tell me you didn't at least skim the message."

"Only the first bit, to make sure she's safe," John admitted, leaning back on the desk as Rory read through the necessarily terse missive.

"She's still at that hotel on Carroll Square, sharing a room with Mia," Rory noted. "And she says—" He paused, went back a few words, and read again. "She says she'll not return to Kit's Diner at all, but means to open her own tea shop."

"Her own place?" John's brows shot up. "I didn't know she had such ambitions."

"Nor I, but she says after some discussion, she and Gideon mean to become partners, of a sort."

"I have trouble seeing Gideon serving tea and cakes," John observed.

"Well, it's not likely he will," Rory said. "Jinna doesn't say much, but it's more that Gideon will be a silent partner to her shop and use his share of the profits for his own business."

"And what business would that be?"

Rory tracked forward along the tape and frowned as he read. "She says he's meaning to become a private facilitator."

"I have no idea what that means."

"Nor I," Rory said with a shrug. "But if it works out, Jinna will be her own boss—no more worrying over whether she'll have a job tomorrow."

"No, but it will be another kind of burden," John observed. "And with a baby on the way—she'll be needing more than financial stability." He met Rory's glance, and for a moment, Rory saw his own doubts reflected in John's eyes. "I won't ask if you've thought about leaving the Errant," he *said at last. "All I ask is, if you do decide to stay with Jinna, you help us find another mechanic." He paused. "And a medic," he added.*

"Well," Rory said, clearing his throat as he looked toward the port, where the skies were purpling with sunset, "its early days, yet, isn't it? No knowing what Jinna will want. Besides, apparently, her own tea shop."

"I think she wants you," John said. "And I know you want her."

"But I also want this," Rory said, turning back to John. "What we've built, what we are building? I want that, too."

"I know," John said, idly picking up an old pocket watch from his desk, sliding the chain through his fingers as he added, "but we can't always have everything we want."

As Eitan followed the others into Satsuke's office, the General slipped around her desk, where she remained standing. As soon as the *Errant* crew was ranged in front of her, she held a hand out to John, who passed over the *cipín* Pascal had given him.

She wasted no time twisting the stick open, and by the time Colonel Tenjin took his place to her right, was engrossed in the message, nothing in her expression indicating what she might be reading.

Then again, as the commander of Special Operations, Kimo Satsuke would likely have exquisite control.

No doubt Galileo Kane—Eitan's ex-lover, and a telepath of exceptional ability—would have challenged that control.

Then again, Leo's constant delving into other people's thoughts had led to a mental breakdown, one from which Eitan doubted he would ever recover.

All of which meant that, as much as Eitan might wish to know what was in the message General Satsuke read—and why that message had led to Conn's death—he would never attempt a glimpse into the general's thoughts.

No matter that, for the first time in his life, such a thing might actually be possible.

———

The Errant *was aloft and on a heading toward Epsilon when Eitan slipped past the quiet galley, the deserted training room, and into the empty medbay.*

None of this was unusual, but after over a week of carrying passengers, there was suddenly much more space . . . more quiet . . . more time to wonder what had happened to Conn back in Adia. Why had he turned against the Colonies? And what, in the name of the First Landers, was in the cipín *that Rory had found?*

"Treading a flowerless meadow," he told himself, heading for the cabinet where Rory stowed the suture kits.

"Which flowerless meadow?" Jagati asked, striding easily into the room.

Eitan looked over his shoulder. "I thought you were on laundry rota?"

"The wash is running," she said with a grimace. "But it looks like I missed a piece." She nodded at his shirt, which was speckled with red-brown dots. "What happened?"

"I may have gotten careless loading up the MBB crawler," Eitan said, pulling out one of the packs, noting they were down to five, which meant another item to add to the supply list. "Pulled a few stitches."

"Ouch," she sympathized. "Why didn't you ask Rory to help?"

"He is communing with his least favorite engine pod," Eitan said, then added, "and you know John is at the helm, and I thought you were busy."

She looked at him, then held out her hand.

Eitan considered the silent offer of assistance. It wasn't as if he couldn't stitch himself up—he could, and had—and often in less comfortable circumstances.

Even as he recalled one of those circumstances, a bead of sweat formed on Jagati's forehead, and the pain and fever Eitan had experienced in a small hut outside of Domino were echoed in her eyes.

Then she let out a hiss and, a heartbeat later, the shutters dropped as she fixed her internal shields in place, which reminded Eitan to likewise fix his own.

In the quiet of the medbay, the two sensitives eyed each other.

"This," he said, dropping the suture pack into Jagati's waiting hand, "could be a problem."

"Ya' think?" Jagati huffed out a breath. "Maybe it's just that my shields weren't strong enough, and . . . the woo is getting wooier."

Eitan's lip twitched at her description. "Neuro-psi scholars throughout Fortune should adopt your terminology," he decided, then in a practiced move, hauled his shirt up over his head with one hand, dropping it onto the cot as he sat down.

At her pointed look, he unbuckled the dagger, as well.

"Dude," she said, "that's like, four out of eight stitches. You didn't notice when it was happening?"

He looked down at his side and grimaced. "It was the tinned salmon that did it, I think."

"Of course." She grumbled something about vat grown sushi and went to the sink to wash her hands.

"Still," Eitan said as she went through the disinfecting routine, "you are not wrong about the . . . wooieness?" He smiled as she glared over her shoulder. "What I mean is that we seem to be connecting more frequently, and more deeply, than when I first joined the crew."

Jagati grunted, snagged the rolling stool from its nook with her foot, and settled next to his bunk before opening the kit. "Weird," she admitted, tearing open the disinfectant. "Weirder that, before you came aboard, I didn't even know I was a sensitive. I just thought what I felt—the sensations—were me interpreting what I saw, heard, smelled; you know, the standard five." She pulled on a pair of gloves and started to clean the reopened wound. "Then you show up, and suddenly I'm not just sensing a random aching knee. It's like a freaking Fujian opera out there. And, and," she continued, opening the tube of numbing gel, "now it goes in reverse too, so other people can get whacked by my emotions." She applied the gel, then glared up at Eitan.

"So you're saying it's my fault?" he asked.

She unwrapped the forceps and addressed the first broken stitch. "Well, it wasn't an issue before."

"True," he said, ignoring the tug of the suture she pulled free. "But it is the same with me, and I have spent time with other sensitives in the past."

There followed a moment of quiet as the ghost of Leo whispered between them.

"Maybe it's not that weird," Jagati broke the silence as she moved on to the next suture. "Maybe it's just two people who don't trust people—"

"That would be you and I?"

"Smart guy," she muttered, dropping the wire onto the tray while Eitan grabbed a gauze pad to pat away the bleeding. "Thanks. Yes, that would be us. We're both—careful about who we let in, right?"

"Hmm," he agreed, watching her hands, steady as ever, as she pulled out the last two sutures.

"Maybe," she ventured, dropping the last wire onto the tray, "there's something about when we do actually trust someone else, and the someone else is also a sensitive, that our shields just don't—" She paused, inserted a fresh suture, and used the forceps to tie it off. "—shield so much."

"Perhaps . . ." he said, then waited for her to insert the next suture. "But I'm not certain that is all." She held out a hand, and he gave her the gauze. "I think—no, I know," he said as she patted at the wound, "I'm sensing more from other people as well. Conn wasn't the first, for me. It isn't much, nor all the time, but I'm sensing fragments of other people's thoughts, even without contact. Especially when you are close by."

"Like I'm what—some smogging amplifier?"

"Or I am," he said. "As you said, you hadn't any idea you were a sensitive before we met."

"Well, hells." Jagati rocked back on the stool, her eyes narrowed in thought. "I can't decide if this is really not good, or if we could cause a ton of trouble with it . . . but, you know, good trouble."

Eitan wondered about that, as well.

But he also knew—too well did he know—that good trouble could turn, quick as a viper, into bad.

Even thinking this, unwanted memories of heat, burning, blood, and screams began to rise.

But under, or over, those memories, he heard a voice—deep, rough, and unknown to him—and with that voice echoes of a child's fear, accompanied by a terrible pain in a very bad place. . .

"Whoa!" *Jagati's head jerked, and she dropped the gauze.*

"Forgive me," *he said, looking away.*

"Same," *she said after letting out a measured breath, then taking another and releasing it.*

"I won't ask about yours if you don't ask about mine," *he offered.*

Jagati's head was down, prepping the last suture, but that had her looking up. "Deal," *she said, the familiar gleam back in her eyes.* "But if this is going to keep happening . . ."

"I think," *he said, filling in the silence,* "short of drugging ourselves into a stupor, we need to find someone with more experience and ask for help. Or," *he paused, let out a breath,* "I could leave. If it becomes too uncomfortable for you."

"Don't be a mammoth turd," *Jagati said, her voice almost a growl.* "I worked way too hard to get you on the crew to let you go. And really," *she added,* "we are a team. No one of us is more important than the others."

"I'm not so certain John would agree with that last," *Eitan said, then paused as Jagati raised the forceps in a poking position over the latest suture.*

"I will do it," *she threatened. Then she let out a loud breath,* "Plus, if you stay, think how much fun we could have if we can figure out how to use this, whatever it is. Like, we could make people laugh at the end of Hamlet . . ."

"That would be a good trick," *Eitan agreed as he privately—very privately—thought that Conn, as he'd been, would have liked Jagati very much.*

CHAPTER 10

Jagati watched Satsuke read the telgram, but nothing in the other woman's expression hinted at what the skinny note contained. Once she'd finished the missive, the general handed the slip of paper to Tenjin and turned to the waiting *Errant* crew. "Thank you for your service," she said, her voice crisp, formal, and about as revealing as a Fujian fog.

"We weren't given much choice in the matter," John pointed out, even as Jagati was opening her mouth to say the same.

"Except for delivering that wee message," Rory offered, rocking back on his heels. "We did have a choice there."

"Yes," the general said, glancing at Rory. "Major Ouellet sent word of your agreement."

"I hope the Corps means to honor that agreement," John said.

"Actually," the general began.

Here we go, Jagati thought, turning back to the general. "Don't tell me. Times are tight. The post-war coffers are thin. The brass is cutting costs on all fronts—"

"In fact," Satsuke cut her off with an utterly neutral glance, "I have been authorized to make you a counteroffer."

"I hope you're not planning to bargain," John began in the mild tone Jagati had learned, long ago, to respect. "Major Ouellet made his offer in good faith, and we honored—"

"I don't bargain," Satsuke again cut in. John's eyes narrowed, but Tenjin glanced up, and while it wasn't quite a smile, Jagati caught a crinkle at the edge of his eyes that hinted at amusement.

"My apologies," John said.

"No apologies necessary." Satsuke met John's gaze, then looked at the rest of the crew. "The fact is, thanks to recent events in Nike, my team has finally managed to deliver proof of what really happened at Nasa."

There was a pause as all four of the *Errant*'s crew went very still, and while they didn't look at each other, Jagati figured they were all wondering what Gideon Quinn had discovered in his investigation into the tragedy.

"It is because of this proof," Satsuke continued, indicating that whatever Gideon had discovered, she wasn't telling, "that I have been granted clearance to—not compensate, as there is no compensation for what each of you endured after Nasa—but at least make some reparation by way of restoring the salaries you all lost since that day, as well as clearing your records of any false accusations." She paused and looked at Eitan. "Your case is a little more complex, as you had been declared KIA."

"Wait," Rory said.

John turned to Eitan. "You never—"

"—told anyone you were alive?" Jagati finished, then grimaced, as it appeared that, no matter her feelings about the man, she and John continued to share at least part of a brain.

"I didn't feel it necessary," Eitan told them. "My tour technically ended while I was in Adia," he explained, "and by the time I escaped and reached the colonies, the war had ended."

"Fair enough," Jagati said, because what else could she say, then looked back to the general. "How—"

"How complicated is Eitan's case?" John asked over Jagati's question.

She had to work, very hard, not to poke him in the arm.

"Not as much as it might have been," the general replied, keeping her attention on Eitan. "Since you waived death benefits to next of kin, it is more a matter of removing your name from the rolls of the lost—though we will leave your tree to grow in the Forest of Memory."

"I am pleased you won't be killing any trees on my account," Eitan murmured.

Satsuke didn't respond but instead picked up a file from her desk, and from that file pulled out a stack of sealed envelopes. "Here are the settlements I arranged," she said and, starting with John, passed one to each member of the crew.

Jagati waited as John unsealed his envelope, pulled out a sheet of paper and what looked like a bank note. He focused on the paper, reading it silently, until—

Whoa!

Jagati tried to reinforce her shielding, but nothing could stop the sandstorm of John's emotions.

Vindication . . . a gaping well of grief . . . the rasping, ever-present shame . . . and so, so much more.

She steeled herself as the tangled weed of emotions tumbled forth, the whole illuminated by a spinning ball of *joyreliefunburdening*.

The whole washed over her, leaving Jagati with the sensation of walking into an amazing smelling kitchen, a thunderstorm, and a forest fire, all at the same time.

Yet, all John showed on the outside was a single muscle contracting on his jaw.

She almost reached out to steady him, but . . . not the time, not the place . . .

And he didn't look like he needed support, anyway.

"*There you are, you little booger.*" *Jagati found the bay leaf in the stew, determined not to lose track of it before serving the one edible dish she had learned to make.*

It was too early to take the leaf out, but if she stood it up in the middle, she wouldn't forget it. She did so, then grinned, as it looked like a tiny shark's fin.

She started pushing it through the stew, then burned her finger, then remembered she still had to start the rice.

This time, she was determined to not mess it up and actually read the instructions on the little card from John's recipe box.

Water just over the knuckle . . .

Which knuckle?

She chuckled to herself as she used the knuckle on her most-used finger.

"Lid on to boil," she murmured as she clanged the lid closed on the rice. "Lid on and wait," she popped the masala's lid into place. Then she noticed the rhythm to that, so she started tapping the spoon on both lids. "Lid on to boil, lid on wait, lid on to boil, lid on wait . . ."

"Keepers witness, Rory. If you're playing silly buggers instead of dealing with the aft port pod, I will confiscate every last drop of Campbell's Best and—oh." John's voice shifted from aggrieved to shocked in the tap of a spoon. "Sorry," he said, turning his eyes upward, as if seeking guidance in the struts. "I thought Rory was in here."

"Well, he's not, is he?" she snapped.

He sighed, and Jagati grimaced because, ever since their lift-off from Upsilon, just breathing the same air as John had become awkward.

Forcing herself to not lift the lid on the rice, she opened the chickpeas to stir, just for something to do, then realized she had lost the bay leaf. "Dammit," she hissed as John crossed the galley.

Jagati focused on the stew, poking around for the MIA bay leaf while he parked himself against the counter. "Can you tell me what's wrong?"

"Nothing," she tried, then glanced over to see him staring at his feet. "Okay, I'm just touchy . . . about choking people on a bay leaf."

"Ah, but we all know Find the Bay Leaf is a time-honored tradition in most Fordian households," John pointed out, probably because he also wanted to avoid talking about the mammoth in the room.

"But you know me," she replied with an almost-smile. "I hate following the crowd."

At which point, both turned toward each other, and their eyes met, and the mammoth came crashing down. And for the space of a few heartbeats, the connection that had driven them toward each other that night in the ice tavern shimmered to life, as warm and vibrant as in the moment.

They each took a step toward the other, and then . . .

"Oy! Something smells fine!"

Rory's voice was like a bucket of ice water over Jagati's head. "Tell me we're havin' that masala, again and I'll be a—ah, oh."

Both John and Jagati turned to where Rory had frozen in the starboard door, one foot still comically in the air. "Masala it is, then." He dropped the foot, then glanced at John. "Great. Grand. So." He paused, shook his head, took a step backwards, spun, and dashed toward the aft ladder.

Hopefully, Jagati thought, back to the aft port pod where he could bash himself in the head with a spanner, sparing her the effort.

Then again, Rory may have done her a favor, because as much as she trusted Captain John Pitte, she wasn't quite as sure about John Pitte, Special Ops officer.

"He's right. Dinner does smell grand," John said, and when Jagati turned, she found he'd returned to his original position. His eyes were fixed on the pot, still bubbling happily as he added, "I seem to recall a recent conversation, where I reminded you that everyone has secrets."

Her spoon froze mid stir, recalling their conversation on the Nike tram, in the middle of the calculator job. "Mmmph." Breathe, stir, breathe, stir. "I guess there are secrets and then there are secrets *. . . and I was expecting . . . well, not expecting . . ." She felt like an ass.*

"You expected I was harboring an illicit gambling addiction? Or perhaps have a hidden collection of Terran soup tins?" he suggested, referring to one of their earliest cargos. "Something less . . . less than this."

There was a hollow feeling in her chest, making his humor fall flat. "I mean, it is not easy to swallow, when the one person . . ." She hissed, put the spoon down, and looked at him. "My bad."

"How?" he asked, still leaning against the counter.

She shrugged. "I get too cocky about what I know about who and why." She shrugged again. "I'll get over it."

"Will you?" he asked. "Can you?" Into the following silence, he added, "Would it be different if I'd learned something about you? Something you'd specifically kept hidden?" The question hung between them, and when she failed to pick it up, he continued. "We all have secrets, Jagati. Some good, some bad, and some because maybe we don't want to think about them. Do those secrets make us less worthy?"

"Less worthy to who?" She echoed the question. "The one keeping them, or the one they need to be kept from?"

"Either," he said. "Both?"

She felt, more than saw, his hand rise as if reaching out before it fell back.

"I suppose that's for you to decide," he said, when she didn't reply. "Either way, I'll be waiting." He straightened from his spot at the counter and started to leave, but at the door of the galley, he paused to add, "I'll see you at dinner."

And then he was gone, leaving Jagati to wonder if she was more afraid of his secrets, or her own.

John was still staring at the letter in his hands when a shocked, "Oy!" had him looking over to see Rory had opened his envelope, and was gaping at the bank note inside, bearing the total of the difference between his higher salary as a gunner's mate on the *Kodiak*, and that as an airman on the *York*.

"It does rather add up, doesn't it?" Eitan barely glanced at his compensation, reminding John that, however he lived now, Eitan had come from wealth.

John looked at Jagati, who shrugged, opened her envelope,

and looked at her compensation for her own demotion to the *Desmos*. Then her eyes widened in genuine surprise. "Wow," she said, then, "Wow," again.

John could appreciate her sentiment, but it was the letter clearing him of any wrongdoing aboard the *Kodiak* that really struck home.

And not only the letter, but the Sol Medal of Valor resting in the bottom corner of the envelope. That . . . was unexpected.

He looked into the envelope again, where the slim box holding the medal rested, a quiet reminder of doing the right thing in the face of an incredible wrong.

To his left, he caught Eitan peering into his envelope, and guessed there was a Crimson Heart inside, at the least.

Finally, John turned to see the general watching him.

"Do not say it is generous," Satsuke said before he could speak. "What happened at Nasa is a stain on the Corps as a whole. This . . ." She gestured toward the envelopes each member of the crew held. ". . . is literally the least we can do by way of restitution. Especially as General Rand is dead and can no longer be prosecuted."

Which none of Gideon's messages had mentioned, but all John said was, "Understood, and appreciated."

"What about Sergeant Jihan?" Jagati asked.

Of course she would ask about Jihan, John thought as Rory gave a start.

Sergeant Wex Jihan had been General Rand's aide de camp and had a few crimes of his own to answer for, beyond stabbing John in the back.

"Unfortunately, Jihan retired from service at the end of the war," Satsuke replied. "We're not sure where he is at this time."

"Worse, as our advocates have explained, it will be difficult to prosecute Sergeant Jihan, as he was following orders," Tenjin added.

Rory, another victim of Jihan's "following orders" shifted, but said nothing.

Satsuke's glance slid from John to the mechanic and back. "As I indicated earlier, this isn't a perfect solution, but it is the best the Corps can do. I am also authorized to offer you your commissions, if you wish to return to the service. Though, having just made a similar offer to another of Nasa's casualties, I believe I already know your answer."

"Thank you, but no," John said.

"Not on your life—respectfully," was Rory's take.

Jagati's snort said it all, and Eitan simply shook his head.

Colonel Tenjin coughed back what might have been a laugh, but Satsuke merely nodded. "As you wish."

At which point everyone stood around for a few moments, as if uncertain what to do next.

"You know what I wish?" Jagati finally tossed into the uncomfortable silence. "I wish for a meal that someone else cooks, serves, and cleans up—and a nonstop flow of alcohol." She waggled her bank note. "On me. Who's in?"

And so, after a few more expressions of mutual appreciation, John and his crew were dismissed.

Once they'd been escorted off base, Rory suggested they head toward the nearby skyway hub that connected Epsilon's districts from above.

"The view's better than the tram or the canals, and we can decide where to get off if we like the looks of it," he said.

"Like we don't spend enough time in the air," Jagati groused, but with a grin. Then she shoved her envelope into her coat's inner pocket. "So, what do we do with the cash?"

"The *Errant* needs some upgrades," John began.

"What, like a crystal drive?" she asked.

"No," John shook his head.

"Can't do crystal." Rory peeked around Eitan's shoulder. "We'd have to lose the liquid aluminium—"

"Aluminum," Jagati muttered.

"—batteries," Rory continued without a break. "We'd also need to rebuild the entire power core . . ." He shook his head. "Might as well buy another airship."

"And we're not buying another airship," John asserted. "But I'm thinking we can replace that aft port pod and upgrade our bact-tank."

"Keepers, yes!"

"And," Rory steamed right over Jagati's cheer, "we could top up on the replacement parts—you know, the bits and bobs that are forever wearing out."

"That may cost the entirety of our windfall," John pointed out.

Eitan shook his head and eased around a party of cadets on their way back to base, ignoring the looks all three sent his way. "I recommend everyone pitch in what they consider fair to the company account." He paused, looked at John. "We do have a company account?"

"Yes," John said.

"Excellent. In that case, we take care of the pod and the bact-tank, add in backups of the most necessary and most used parts, and set the rest aside for potential investments."

"You said something about diversifying before." John recalled a previous discussion with Eitan about updating Errant Freight's business plan. Since, to that point, Errant Freight's business plan had been less a plan and more a "let's buy an airship and see what happens," it could only be an improvement.

"I guess you weren't talking about betting on the Fujian marathon?" Jagati guessed.

"I was not." Eitan shot her a smile. "I meant we should keep an eye out for promising businesses on the ground. Invest for a percentage of the gross." Eitan looked at Rory. "Something like what Gideon is doing with Jinna's tea shop."

"I'm game, as long as you still get the bact-tank," Jagati said. "Besides the glory of taking a shower longer than three minutes, having functioning facilities will make it easier to take on more passengers."

"*You* want to take on more passengers?" Rory asked, shocked.

"What?" She shrugged. "It didn't entirely suck swamp water this time."

"This time," Eitan echoed. "Not every party will be as charming as the doctors."

"Opposite argument, we probably won't get another spy in the mix," Rory said, his voice dropping, though there was no one else nearby. "I mean, how many are out there?"

"No one knows," John said, taking a breath perfumed by the pine trees lining the path, "which is rather the point."

"Whatever. I just want to have water available when I need water," Jagati said.

"Bact-tank and engine pod," Rory echoed, producing a notepad and pencil from somewhere.

"I wouldn't recommend we start throwing money around at the first opportunity, either," Eitan said. "We should wait for something that has legs and feels right for us."

"Like the tea shop," Rory echoed Eitan's earlier statement.

"I also wouldn't recommend going into competition with Jinna—" Eitan began.

"Not if you value your life," Jagati said.

"—but there may be other opportunities—something that supports both our financial goals and gives someone else a chance they might not otherwise have."

John eased back a few steps, watching the others as they bent their heads over Rory's pad.

Jagati was laughing and slapping Rory on the shoulder, and all three were walking in sync.

Knowing his crew, John doubted such harmony would last, but he allowed himself to enjoy the moment.

He felt the weight of the letter in his breast pocket, and thought of how it had come to be there.

General Satsuke had been right when she said there could never be true compensation for Nasa, but, for now at least, it was enough.

The *Errant* Crew Will Return in *Fortune's Lost*.
For now, turn the page to see what Gideon Quinn, Mia, and Elvis are getting up to in *Fortune's Fool*.

PREVIEW:
FORTUNE'S FOOL

FORTUNE CHRONICLES 3

CHAPTER 1

Lower Cadbury-Outer 9th District
Nike City, Avon
United Colonies of Fortune
April 18, 1449 After Landing

HIS LONG COAT WHIPPING IN THE SPRING WINDS, Gideon Quinn came to a stop before a ramshackle building in Lower Cadbury.

Because the afternoon suns were shining with unusual vigor, he had to squint up at the faded sign nailed over the building's entrance.

"A Fine Mess," he read aloud, then grinned at the reptilian snort from the draco on his right shoulder. "Yeah, not much to look at," he agreed, giving Elvis a soothing scritch under his chin. "But we've seen worse."

A second snort indicated Elvis wasn't sure they had.

Since Elvis might be right, Gideon checked the lay of the collapsable baton under his left sleeve.

The baton, fondly named Lulu, had been created as payment

for Gideon's first official job as a private facilitator. Iliana, the client in question, was a designer of small devices and weapons.

She also, as Gideon learned after closing the case, brewed a mean cup of tea.

Assured his weapon of choice was locked and loaded in the spring holster designed by a friend, Gideon hauled the creaking door open and entered A Fine Mess, where he took a moment to allow his vision to adjust to the dim interior, then another to appreciate truth in advertising.

Taking in the odors of cheap booze and stale sweat, he continued into the pub, where flickering overheads failed to soften scorched walls pocked by gaping shutters.

The furniture he passed was of the "found on a curb" design, and the clientele draped in clothes as threadbare as their faces were worn.

But as he wound through the tables, Gideon overheard the same easy rumbles of conversation he'd expect in any other tavern, and a rattle of dice drew his eyes to a game of Colonists of Mercedes, where the last roll netted a player three beds of crystal, which she immediately used to build an airship.

By this time there were more than a few speculative gazes tracking his path, as well as a non-zero number of hands reaching for what might be concealed weapons.

Accustomed to this level of suspicion, Gideon clicked his tongue and murmured, *"High road."*

At the prompt, Elvis, his talons rasping against the pauldron on which he rested, leapt up, and with a single flap of his wings settled on the smoke stained rafters.

As often occurred when Gideon deployed Elvis, a series of gasps and sighs followed in the draco's wake, easing the overall tension in the room.

Or, most of the tension, as Gideon noted a fellow holding down a table at the rear of the pub who didn't seem the least interested in the draco, but was more than ready to meet Gideon's gaze.

A dagger of sunslight slashed through a nearby shutter to spark off the blood red studs in the man's ears, and highlighting a deep scar running down one side of his deep umber face.

And while there was nothing overtly threatening about the man, he sat with the kind of readiness Gideon associated with a natural fighter.

Curious, but as the bear dog in a waterman's clothing wasn't the reason Gideon had come to A Fine Mess, he offered a nod of greeting-slash-neutrality.

The bear dog's lip twitched, but he offered a reciprocal nod, and Gideon continued on to the bar where an individual with a neat goatee and a memory of hair ringing his scalp stood wiping a glass.

Easing up alongside a skeletal figure half a head shorter than himself, Gideon aimed his attention to the trio on his right, all half a head taller. "Rolf," he greeted the nearest giant. "Ulf, Freya." He tapped his heart in a quick Corps salute for the Stolichnayan triplets who, after an unfortunate first meeting, had proven to be both solid allies and good friends.

"Good day, Gideon," Ulf replied, as all three raised their glasses in greeting.

"What are you guys doing here?" he asked, glancing at the diminished bottle they shared. "I thought you'd all found work at the meat-growing plant."

Rolf shifted, clearly uncomfortable. "We did have this job, but—"

"There was a problem with Rolf mixing the makings of the poultry with the makings of the pork," Freya cut in, throwing her brother a disgusted look.

"Oh," Gideon said, while someone at a nearby table made a retching noise. He turned to Rolf. "*Why?*"

"I was thinking it would make the recipe for Chicken Tolstoy easier. No need to wrap the chicken bits around the ham bits, yes?"

"No," Freya said.

"Here, here," called one of the Colonists of Mercedes players.

"Gotta go with Freya on this one," Gideon agreed.

"So did the manager of the plant." Rolf sighed into his booze.

"So, the manager fired all of you?" Gideon asked.

"Not quite," Ulf said.

"First, she is only firing Rolf," Freya began.

"But then Ulf tried to prove how it was maybe not such a bad idea," Rolf joined in.

"By mixing the pork into the aurochs," Freya picked up the thread again.

"Like kebobs," Ulf explained.

The bartender paused mid-swipe of his glass. "Seriously?"

"Okay, so no meat processing for you," Gideon said to Ulf and Rolf. "Or cooking, I think." Then he focused on Freya. "Did you get the boot, too?"

"No one gives me the boot," that young woman said with a sniff. "I quit, in solidarity with my idiot brothers."

"Way to stick it to the Man."

"But the meat-plant manager is non-binary," Ulf told Gideon.

Some things, Gideon thought, weren't worth explaining. "It's a Fordian thing," he said. "Anyway, sorry about the jobs."

"There will be other jobs." Freya asserted calmly. "But where is Mia?" She leaned forward as Ulf poured more liquor into all their glasses. "She is still your apprentice, no?"

"She is still my apprentice, yes. But she's an apprentice with a geography lesson to finish, so she's back at the office."

"And are you liking the place on Doyle Street?" Rolf asked.

"I think it'll suit," Gideon said. "Mia and Jinna both like it a lot."

"Doyle . . . " A drinker at one of the nearby tables mused over the street name while the hook which replaced his right hand tapped the table. "Ain't that the street what burned to ashes when that morph house went up in flames?"

"Nah, you're thinking of Baudelaire Street," another patron intoned through a beard so thick, it could serve as a scarf.

"Not Baudelaire, neither," a third opined. "'Twas Byron."

"Morph houses are always catching fire on Byron," the barkeep tossed in.

"Aye, Doyle's a nice little spot," a woman from the Mercedes table agreed. "If you don't mind living off the crystal grid. And there's a nice bookshop down t'end of the street," she added, taking a drag from her pipe.

"Doyle isn't very populated," Gideon regained hold of the conversation and aimed it at the triplets. "But the cross streets, Cornwell and Butler, have a lot of traffic, so Jinna's confident the tea shop will do well."

"Mama was impressed that you and Jinna would be going into partnership together, you with your facilitating and Jinna with her cookery," Freya said.

"Speaking of, how goes the facilitating?"

At Ulf's question, Gideon felt a jerk of motion from the skeletal man at his left. "It's interesting," he determined, focusing on the triplets.

"As interesting as vat-grown Chicken Tolstoy?" Freya asked.

"Nothing will ever be that interesting," Gideon determined. "But with the facilitating, the biggest issue is while there are plenty who need my services, most of them aren't what you'd call rolling in starbucks."

"But how are you being paid?"

"In trade, for the most part," Gideon told Rolf. "Curtains, dishes, some bits of furniture. One of our clients is an engraver, and he paid up by making a sign for the office."

A sign he hadn't yet hung, he recalled with a twinge of guilt.

I'll get to it, he told himself.

You keep saying that, his self said back. *And yet . . .*

"And lots of foodstuffs," he continued, drowning out the internal commentary. "Lots. Enough that Jinna's been able to test an apiary's worth of recipes for MacGuffin's. That's what she's naming the shop."

"We know," Rolf said with a quick grin. "We visited Jinna last week, and she let us taste her Man in the High Cassoulet."

"That's pretty good," Gideon admitted. "But you haven't lived until you've tried her Penne from Heaven."

The bartender made a choking sound.

"And is Jinna well?" Freya asked.

"Good. She's . . . good."

"When we see her last, she is looking, ah—" Rolf made a mounding gesture over his stomach.

"Ready to pop," Ulf filled in.

"She's pretty eager to get MacGuffin's up and running before the baby gets here," Gideon said.

"We could help," Ulf suggested. "Since we are not at the meat-growing plant."

"Sure," Gideon said. "Just, you know, don't mention the Chicken Tolstoy."

At which point a gentle clearing of a throat had him turning to face the bartender.

"Sorry to interrupt," he said to Gideon, "but did you plan to order a drink?"

"Do I look suicidal?"

"That's just hurtful," the bartender replied over Ulf's bark of a laugh.

Freya leaned forward on her elbows. "Gideon must have learned about the pool."

"Can't say that I have," Gideon replied.

"There is no pool," the bartender said.

"Yes, there is," Ulf asserted, slapping his hand on the bar with a meat-like thud. "I know this because we started it." He lifted his hand from the bar with a sucking sound as his skin pulled free from whatever substance coated the surface. "We three," he waved the sticky palm at his siblings, "are making book on how many drinks of Msr Martin Soong's booze it would take to put a person in hospital."

All across the room, Gideon heard glasses thudding and chairs creaking as bodies turned towards the bar.

"And how is the pool going?" he asked into the fresh silence.

"Not so good," Freya admitted.

"We three are the only ones to enter," Ulf explained.

"And since we are seeing no one keeling over . . . " Rolf added.

"Perhaps we find something else to be betting on," Freya concluded.

"Good plan," Gideon offered as all three clinked glasses and downed their theoretically hazardous liquor.

While the Ohmdahls played Stoli roulette with their beverages, the bartender, presumably Msr Martin Soong, let out a long-suffering sigh, then addressed Gideon. "If you haven't come for a drink, then why, may I ask, are you here?"

"I'm looking for someone," Gideon told him. "A guy named Jer Hardcastle."

Martin's angular brows angled more. "Have you ever heard that ancient Earth ditty? The one about the place where everyone knows your name?"

"Sure." Just hearing Martin describe the song started up an echo in Gideon's head. "A guy in my company used to sing it. Until the rest of us made him stop."

"Yes. Well. My point is, this place is the opposite of the place in that song. Most people here don't want anyone to know their name."

"Never say it, Martin!" the woman from the Mercedes table called.

Martin grimaced a smile, then leaned closer to quietly add, "I'd be happier if none of them knew my name, so I'm afraid I don't know this Hardrook."

"Castle. Hardcastle," Gideon corrected.

"Rook, castle, pawn . . . " Martin straightened. "Whoever he is, I can't help you."

Which was when Elvis let out a low-throated keen, drawing Gideon's attention to the skeletal man at his left, and the metallic gleam of a stiletto, already in motion.

End of preview.

Fortune's Fool is now available.

Acknowledgments

Gratitude to Lori Drake and Cameron Coral for the morning writing/editing sessions, as well as Lori Diederich and Youness Elh for making the Fortune Chronicles readable and pretty, respectively.

Thanks, always to our families, both blood and chosen, and thanks especially to Himself for the leap of faith that led us, at long last, home.

And of course a huge shout out to **all of you**! We've said it before, but the truth is, without readers, stories are merely lonely echoes in the void.

We're especially grateful everyone who takes time **to leave a review,** which helps other readers who love character-driven adventures discover the wild world of Fortune.

About the Authors

A believer in the fun of fiction, Kathleen uses her history in theatre and fight choreography to create immersive adventures for fellow lovers of found families, outrageous escapades, and chaotic choices.

In addition to keeping the *Errant* crew flying, Kelley recently returned from five years of teaching acting in Shanghai. She now serves as an adjunct professor, teaching voice and directing at Mary Baldwin University in Staunton, Va. During the summers she teaches acting for the New School at New York University.

Both Kathleen and Kelley can be found hanging out at Ream Stories, growing more outrageous adventures featuring flawed heroes, chosen families, and all the snark you care to entertain.*

*Don't let the placid smiles fool you. The two K's have Statler and Waldorfed their way through many a stuffy gathering.

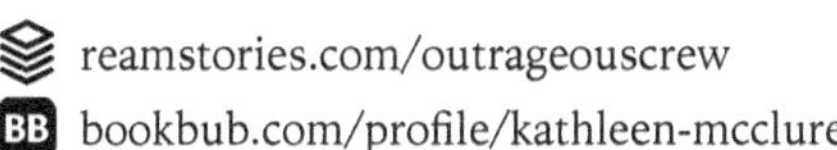

reamstories.com/outrageouscrew
bookbub.com/profile/kathleen-mcclure

MORE OUTRAGEOUS FICTION

THE FORTUNE CHRONICLES

Soldier of Fortune

Fortune's Fallen

Outrageous Fortune

Change of Fortune

Fortune's Fool

THE ZODIAC FILES

The Gemini Hustle

The Libra Gambit

www.ingramcontent.com/pod-product-compliance
Lightning Source LLC
Chambersburg PA
CBHW021718190726
48289CB00008B/2589